# GIRL U̶N̶D̶

'get wants a quiet life, but a boy
d Menzies makes her an offer she
t refuse.

a daring plan – to rescue two kids,
al and Bibi, from a desert
ention centre.

n Bridget and Menzies pull off their
first jailbreak, or will they end up
ind bars too?

# GIRL
# UNDERGROUND

Morris Gleitzman

First published in Great Britain in 2005
by
Puffin Books
This Large Print edition published by
BBC Audiobooks
by arrangement with
Penguin Books Ltd 2007

ISBN 978 1405 662611

British Library Cataloguing in Publication Data available

Printed and bound in Great Britain by
Antony Rowe Ltd., Chippenham, Wiltshire

For all the Jamals and Bibis

# CHAPTER ONE

I should be arrested for this.

The time is approximately 4.17 p.m. and I'm proceeding in an easterly direction along a corridor in one of Australia's most seriously top-notch boarding schools.

'Look at this floor,' says Mum. 'Genuine marble.'

'These wall panels are oak,' says Dad. 'Real wood.'

'Solid brass chandeliers,' says Uncle Grub, his leather jacket creaking as he gazes upwards. 'Pity I didn't bring the van.'

I know I should be thrilled like they are. I wish I was.

But instead I just feel anxious.

We walk past huge sideboards with genuine priceless porcelain vases on them. We stare up at genuine oil paintings of famous historical people who went to this school.

'That'll be you, Bridget,' says Dad, pointing up at a dead Prime Minister.

I know I should be grateful. Mum and Dad have worked incredibly hard to send me to this school. I should feel lucky and privileged, like the headmaster said just now when he was showing us around.

It's a crime not to.

But I don't feel grateful, I feel close to panic. I'm terrified Uncle Grub's going to nick one of the vases.

I glance up and down the corridor. No security cameras. No infra-red burglar alarms. There's a photocopier over there that's not even chained to the wall. This place is just asking for it.

Uncle Grub is stroking a vase.

'Awesome crockery,' he says.

'George,' murmurs Mum. 'Behave.'

I know what she's saying. She's warning Uncle Grub that if he fingers anything and gets sprung and we end up in a high speed police chase across the school grounds and my education suffers, she'll do him.

'Little suggestion, Grub,' says Dad. 'If you go and warm the car up for us, you won't be tempted, eh?'

'I was only looking,' mutters Uncle

Grub.

The expression on Dad's face doesn't change. Dad might be a criminal, but he doesn't believe in stealing.

Now Mum and Dad are on the case I feel a bit better. I take a deep breath and try to calm down. It's a stressful experience, being sent to boarding school.

Uncle Grub gives me a kiss on the head.

'Study hard, gorgeous,' he says. 'Show those posh mongrels what you're made of.'

He strolls off towards the carpark.

'Thanks, Uncle Grub,' I say.

No need to panic.

Not yet.

'Wish I'd gone to a school like this,' says Dad. 'Be a different person if I had.'

Mum kisses him on the cheek. She looks really pretty in her new frock, specially with her hair in ringlets and the sleeves covering her tattoos.

'I love you just the way you are,' she says to Dad as we step outside into the sunshine. She means it too, even though Dad's wearing a yellow shirt with a blue suit.

Dad grabs Mum on the bottom and they both laugh.

I look anxiously around the school grounds. Other kids and their parents are strolling about, mostly wearing tennis clothes with sweaters knotted over their shoulders.

None of them are looking at us.

Not yet.

I peer over towards the carpark, trying to see if Uncle Grub is getting into our car or someone else's.

'Check this,' says Dad proudly, patting the wall of an old building. 'Genuine sandstone.'

Suddenly I can't keep quiet any longer. I hate being a squealer, specially on my first day, but I can't stop myself.

'I don't want to go to this school,' I say quietly.

Mum and Dad stare at me, shocked. Then Mum gives me a hug.

'I know, love,' she says. 'It's all new and scary. But you'll feel different

4

when you've made some friends.'

I sigh.

Friends?

Me?

Dream on.

Dad puts his arm round me too. 'By the time we see you at parents' night tomorrow you'll be loving it here,' he says. 'Trust me.'

'This school,' says Mum, 'is going to give you everything me and Dad didn't have.'

I nod sadly.

I can't do it to them. They spent months choosing this place. Mum cancelled the plastic surgery on her tattoos so they could afford the fees. How can I tell them I'd rather be going into Mrs Posnick's class at my old school?

'You've got to admit,' says Mum, giving me another squeeze, 'this place is better than your old school.'

I nod again.

But I don't mean it.

My old school's only ten minutes from home by foot. The uniform's a comfortable t-shirt instead of this scratchy blazer. And the teachers and kids are fantastic. Nobody tries to push you into being their friend. If you want to keep to yourself so nobody finds out your family are criminals, you can.

This school is crawling with the kids of lawyers and judges and commissioners of police. If they find out what Mum and Dad do, we're sunk.

I open my mouth to tell Mum and Dad that sending me here is putting our whole family at risk and that they're making a terrible mistake.

But I don't.

Their faces are so hopeful.

I remember how miserable they were when Gavin got put away for shoplifting. I'm their only other kid. I can't hurt them too. I have to try and get through the next seven years.

Somehow.

For them.

As I'm thinking this, Dad steers me over to a complete stranger.

'S'cuse me,' says Dad, blocking the stranger's path. 'I'm Len White. You a teacher?'

The stranger, a tall skinny bloke with a beaky face and a bundle of folders under his arm, looks at me and Mum and Dad about twice each.

'Creely,' he says. 'Science and Personal Development.'

Dad pumps Mr Creely's hand. Mr Creely gives him a thin smile.

'This is my daughter Bridget,' says Dad. 'She's just starting in year six. Bridget's a very sensitive and top-notch young person. If you could see your way clear to helping her settle in, I would be personally very grateful.'

Mr Creely gives me the thin smile.

'We regard every student as sensitive and er, top-notch,' he says. 'Every one of them will receive the very best care and support. As young Bridget will discover at her first assembly tomorrow morning.'

Dad reaches into his inside pocket.

With a jolt of panic I realise what he's going to do.

No, Dad, I plead silently. Not here.

It's too late.

Dad pulls a plastic object out of his pocket and presses it into Mr Creely's hand.

'Bulgarian gameboy,' says Dad. 'Seriously top-notch quality. With my compliments.'

Mr Creely stares at the gameboy, horrified. 'Thank you,' he says. 'But I couldn't possibly . . .'

'Don't fret,' says Dad. 'I've got a warehouse full of 'em. Keep a friendly eye on Bridget for me and I'll sling you an Iraqi blender next visit.'

I pray Mr Creely doesn't ask to see the import documents for the gameboy. I'm not sure if the Bulgarian businessmen Dad deals with can even write.

'Um, thank you,' mutters Mr Creely and hurries away.

'Nice bloke,' says Dad, ruffling my hair.

Mum is frowning at Dad's jacket pocket. I can see she's wondering what else he's brought along from the warehouse.

'We should probably be thinking about going, love,' says Mum to me. 'Would you like us to take you back to your room and say goodbye there?'

8

'No thanks,' I say. 'The carpark's fine.'

I just want to get them out of here before Dad tries to give a set of Algerian hair-curlers to a passing high court judge.

We go over to the car. Mum spends a long time hugging me and saying loving things. Normally I'd be glowing with happiness, but I just can't concentrate, not while we're standing next to the only Mercedes in the carpark with dents and a spoiler and flared mudguards. It's not Dad's fault. Uncle Grub gave it to him. In our family we believe it's rude to criticise presents or get them panel-beaten.

Dad says lots of loving things too, and gives me a Turkish personal organiser.

Uncle Grub waves at me through the car window.

Then they drive away.

I wave back, trying to hold the tears in so I won't draw attention to myself.

I'm sad because they're going, but I'm even sadder because I know the real reason Mum and Dad are paying a fortune to send me to a boarding school that's only an hour by car or school bus from our place.

They think if they keep me out of the house I won't end up like them.

Crims.

Which is hard for me because they're kind and generous and good and I love them and I do want to end up like them.

They've gone.

I'd better get inside before other parents start talking to me.

Hang on, what's that cloud of dust coming through the school gates? It's a car going really fast. Spraying gravel onto the flowerbeds. Is it them rushing back so Dad can give me an Israeli calculator?

Oh no.

It's something even worse and it's heading straight for me.

A police car.

# CHAPTER TWO

I stand frozen as the police car hurtles towards me along the school driveway.

Are we nicked already?

Did Mr Creely see the fake serial number on the gameboy? Did he spot that the Nintendo logo is in Bulgarian? Did he call the police to interrogate me in front of all the other parents and kids till I crack in the glare of their silver jewellery and gold watches and dob Mum and Dad in?

I'm not hanging around to find out.

I sprint across the carpark and along the side of the library building, desperately looking for a place to hide. There must be a cellar around here where the librarian puts all the books with rude words in them.

A drain.

A ditch.

Anything.

I glance over my shoulder to see if the police are chasing me on foot. They're not. They're not chasing me at all. They're not even looking in my direction. They don't seem the slightest bit interested in me helping them with their enquiries.

Wobbly with relief, I pretend to tie my shoelace so I can see what they're up to.

The police car is parked outside the school office. Two policemen are helping a kid out of the back seat. He's wearing a school blazer. The policemen escort him into the office. One of them carries the kid's suitcase.

I realise I've been staring about ten times longer than it takes to tie a shoelace, so I stand up and hurry over to the building my room is in.

As I climb the stone steps my thoughts are going faster than a Bulgarian food processor, the turbo model.

Why was that kid in the police car?

Did he escape last term and they've only just recaptured him?

Or does he just know someone in the police force?

Dad used to sell toilets to a property developer who made such big donations to the police widows and orphans fund that the police used to help him paint his beach house and sometimes drive his kids to judo.

I turn the corner at the top of the steps.

The upstairs corridor is full of kids and parents dragging luggage into rooms and admiring each other's tans. Most of them look like they've known each other since year four. I try to look as though I've been here since year four as well. It's not easy because I can't remember where my room is.

There it is.

The one with the loud voices coming out if it. Oh no.

My room mates must have arrived.

I pause outside the door and try to prepare myself for questioning. Luckily I've got good genes for being questioned. Dad was questioned by the police for two hours once and the only thing he admitted was that fish gives him wind.

I just wish I could tell the truth about Mum and Dad's import business. OK, it's illegal, but at least it means they can sell cheap appliances to people who can't afford expensive ones.

Too risky.

I go in.

'G'day,' I say. 'I'm Bridget.'

For a weird moment I think I'm sharing the room with triplets. The three girls sitting on their beds have all got exactly the same hairstyle. Long and straight except for a slight curl under their chins.

They look up at me and don't smile. For a second I think I'm going to have to fight them. Then they do smile.

I realise they were just startled by my hair. Mum's hairdresser Chervawn gave me a really spiky haircut yesterday. I just wanted a trim, but Chervawn owes us heaps of haircuts after Dad gave her eighty litres of Taiwanese conditioner.

'Hello,' says one of the girls. 'Welcome to the stables.'

'We call this room the stables cause we've all got horses,' says another of the girls.

'Have you got a horse?' says the third girl.

I can see they're not triplets now. They've all got different-shaped noses and eyes and their pimples are in different places.

I tell them I don't actually own a horse but I have sat on a Melbourne Cup winner. Uncle Ray had it at his place the day before the race to give it some special injections. I don't tell them that bit.

The girls are very impressed and introduce themselves. Their names are Chantelle, Antoinette and Veuve. They don't have French accents, but they can still pronounce their names really well.

The good thing is they'd much rather talk about horses than parents.

'This is Gandalf,' says Chantelle, holding out a photo to me. 'He's sooo cute. Poor thing, he'll be so lonely locked in those boarding stables without me.'

'Same with Brad,' says Antoinette, holding out a photo too. 'During term he paces around that paddock like he's in a jail cell. The only thing that cheers him up is when Dad gives him strawberries.'

I'm very tempted to tell them that a jail cell is quite a bit smaller than a paddock, and that it's even worse having a brother locked up than a horse. I manage not to. Instead I make a mental note to take Gavin some strawberries.

Veuve is fiddling with the lock on her suitcase. She pushes the case onto the floor and swears at it. I'm a bit shocked. Mum and Dad don't like swearing.

'I've lost the key and I can't get it open,' wails Veuve.

Antoinette and Chantelle grin at each other. 'Oh no,' says Antoinette. 'A whole term in the same undies.'

Veuve gives Antoinette a scornful look.

'I can buy more clothes and stuff,' she says. Then her face crumples. 'All my photos of Muffy are in there. He looks sooo cute in his new saddle.'

I can see she's really upset.

Without thinking I drop to my knees in front of the suitcase. Typical expensive flash luggage with a lock that wouldn't keep a mosquito out.

16

Dad's cousin Ollie is an airport baggage handler and he showed me how if you jam a pen into the lock and bash the lid a certain way, ninety-eight percent of suitcases will fly open before you can say, 'Sorry madam, your luggage is on a plane to Gympie.'

I jam a pen into the lock and bash the lid. It flies open.

Then I realise what I've done.

Veuve and Chantelle and Antoinette are staring at me, mouths open as wide as the suitcase.

Without saying a word, I've almost dobbed Mum and Dad in. I might as well be wearing a t-shirt that says 'my lot are all crims'.

I try not to think how many judges Antoinette, Veuve and Chantelle have got in their families. Or dads who play golf with judges. Or mums who sell judges their helicopters.

I stand up.

'S'cuse me,' I say. 'I've just remembered I need to be somewhere else.'

I hurry out of the room, glad I didn't accept the matching set of Romanian

17

picnic baskets Dad wanted to give me for luggage. If my room mates want to break into my bag to check for stolen goods, they'll have to get through an ex-army kitbag with a triple-tumbler brass padlock and they won't be able to.

I run down the corridor and down the stairs. I don't know where I'm going.

All I know is I want to be alone. It's the only safe place for me to be in this school.

Mum and Dad sent me here because they think a posh expensive school will keep me out of jail. It's a very kind thought, but pretty dopey because now I've got to concentrate day and night to keep *them* out of jail.


# CHAPTER THREE

As I run across the courtyard lawn a loud bell rings.

For a panicked second I think it's an alarm bell.

*Crim in the school.*
*She's trying to hide.*
*Get her.*

Then I remember it's just the meal bell. There was a bell demonstration this morning while I was enrolling. Short bell for end of lesson, medium bell for assembly, long bell for mealtimes, bell that sounds a bit like Dad's Latvian Christmas door chimes for church.

Suddenly the courtyard is full of kids, jostling and yelling as they head for the dining hall.

I duck into a stairwell, down behind some mop buckets under the stairs. I'm hungry, but I'd rather go without than have to make small talk with three hundred sons and daughters of families with burglar alarms.

Once everyone's in the dining hall, I'll creep back to my room, eat some of the Bulgarian chocolate biscuits Dad packed in my bag, and be in bed asleep by the time my room mates get back from dinner.

First, though, I want to spend a bit of time with Gavin.

I pull his latest letter out of my pocket.

Gavin writes really good letters. The spelling's not always spot on, but the feelings are. When I read how much he loves us all and misses us and can't wait to get out of prison, tears come to my eyes. And now I'm in this place I know even more how he feels.

I read Gavin's letter three times behind the mop buckets until my leg starts to cramp. Then I stand up, peering out across the courtyard.

All clear.

Suddenly, down the corridor behind me, I hear a boy swearing.

This is incredible. If Mum and Dad knew how much swearing goes on here, I reckon they'd have second thoughts about this place.

I'm about to sprint across the courtyard to my building when the boy starts swearing even louder. There's something in his voice that makes me stop and listen. As well as sounding angry, he also sounds sad and frustrated and trapped.

Just like me.

I creep along the corridor, towards the voice. Go back, I say to myself as I get closer. Go back to your room and go to bed.

I ignore myself.

Gavin reckons he ignored himself the day he got caught. Don't nick the cuckoo clock, he said to himself. It's too big to fit under your coat. But he ignored himself and the cuckoo went off as he was creeping out through Men's Underwear.

The swearing is coming from inside that room. I stand outside the door, listening.

That sounds like a very sad, very upset person in there.

Don't knock, I tell myself.

I knock.

The door isn't locked. It isn't even latched. It swings open.

I stare.

A boy is sitting at a desk, an untouched meal on a plate in front of him, reading a letter with the unhappiest face I've seen in this school since I caught my own reflection in Dad's rear vision mirror.

It's the boy from the police car.

He looks up.

'Are you OK?' I say.

He stares at me.

'Who are you?' he says.

'Bridget,' I say. 'Bridget White.' We don't mind giving our family name now since Dad changed it a few years ago.

I can't take my eyes off the boy's letter. That's what's making him sad, I just know it. The letter.

'What do you want?' says the boy. He's got big round glasses and a startled expression. He doesn't look like a swearer.

'You sounded upset,' I say. 'I was worried.'

He looks at me for a bit. I can see he's a worrier too.

'You shouldn't be here,' he says at last. 'This is the boys' building. If you get caught here we'll both be in for it.'

I take his point. There was a bit in the school rules about what'll happen to kids who go into the other lot's building.

'The adults are all in the dining hall,' I say, just to show him I don't scare easily.

'My bodyguard isn't,' says the boy.

I stare at him. Then I look around the room. Only one bed. No bodyguard.

I look back at the boy. If he's got a bodyguard, why did he come to school in a police car?

What a shame. He seemed like a nice person. He didn't seem like a crackpot or a liar.

Not till now.

As I hurry out of the building and across the courtyard, I try not to be too hard on myself.

It's what happens, I tell myself. You're at a new school and feeling lonely. You see a kid with a police escort and a private room and an upsetting letter. You start to think you've got things in common with him. You start to think that just possibly here's a person you could risk making friends with.

You completely forget that this is an exclusive top-notch school. That the chance of two kids here both having crim dads is about as unlikely as a

23

Mongolian deep-fryer having two chip baskets.

## CHAPTER FOUR

I've never felt lonely sharing a room with three other people before.

When I went camping with Mum and Dad and Uncle Grub, I didn't feel lonely once. Not even when the police came and took Dad and Uncle Grub off for questioning because our cabin was full of toasters. Me and Mum wrapped ourselves in blankets and talked all night and made toast.

I felt a bit worried, but not lonely.

Not like here.

OK, my room mates have tried to be friendly. When they got back from dinner just now and saw I was already in bed, they did try to make conversation.

'Hey, Bridget,' said Antoinette. 'Where did you learn that trick with the pen?'

'Do your folks make crime movies?'

24

said Chantelle.

'Or luggage?' said Veuve.

It was kind, but it was also just what I'd feared. Too much friendliness. I don't think I've got good genes for being questioned after all.

I muttered something about being tired and pulled the covers over my head. That was about two hours ago.

The girls weren't offended. They just started talking about horses. I thought they'd never shut up and go to sleep. One more whisper about Muffy's new saddle or Brad's cute fetlocks or the colour of Gandalf's poo and I'd have jumped out of bed and committed an assault with menaces on their photo albums.

Just as well I didn't or they'd have seen I'm still wearing my school uniform and shoes.

I think they're asleep now.

Antoinette's breathing heavily and Veuve's snoring and Chantelle's making a noise with her mouth like a horse drinking.

Now's my chance to get out of here and go home and tell Mum and Dad that I've given this school a go for their sakes but that it's just too dangerous. They'll understand when I explain to them about the stupid mistake I made with Veuve's bag and about the relentless questioning I'll be suffering over the next seven years. They'll understand why I have to leave and why they mustn't come to parents' night tomorrow.

They've got to.

I slip out of bed.

Should I try and take my luggage with me? No, learn from Gavin's mistake. You never get away if you're too loaded down. He reckons he could have outrun the store detectives if it hadn't been for the jaffle maker in his coat pocket.

Quietly I lift my bag onto my bed, pull the covers over it and head for the door.

I silently thank Gavin for the birthday present he gave me when I was seven. At the time I didn't think it was much of a present from a big brother, being taught how to walk across a room in pitch darkness without tripping over shoes or books, but now I do.

Better than a fairy dress any day.

I slip out of the room, hurry along the passage and down the stairs.

The tricky bit is at the bottom. The front door is locked, and Ms Hummer the boarding mistress has her room right next to it.

I have to be quiet.

Luckily Dad's cousin Ollie knew I didn't want a fairy dress for my birthday this year either. He gave me something much more useful. A master key, guaranteed to open ninety-eight percent of deadlocks before you can say, 'Help I've been burgled.'

I slide the key into the lock, jiggling it gently like Uncle Ollie showed me.

I turn it and the door clicks open.

I pause, listening for the sound of Ms Hummer waking up and groping for her slippers and torch and detention book.

Nothing.

I step out into the cool night air and carefully lock the door behind me.

Don't want burglars getting in.

Then I set off towards the school gates, keeping on the grass so I don't crunch on the gravel. I can see the gates up ahead in the moonlight. Beyond that, the open road. I don't even know which direction the local town is or how far I have to walk to get to the nearest station or bus stop.

Doesn't matter. I've got all night. Ms Hummer is meant to do bed checks, but I overheard the girls saying she hardly ever does.

I've got plenty of time to get home and then beg Mum and Dad to let me stay there if I promise to choose a career other than crime.

I climb up the school gates. From the top I peer along the road in both directions, trying to see a signpost.

Nothing.

Dad's always complaining about the lack of signposts on roads. He reckons people in local government keep the signpost money for themselves to buy over-priced Japanese electrical goods.

I decide to go to the right. When Gavin was sprung with the cuckoo clock he tried to go to the left through

Men's Cosmetics and was arrested.

Suddenly I'm dazzled by a light.

A torch, shining in my face.

A hand grabs my leg and drags me backwards off the gate. I fall onto the gravel driveway and it really hurts.

Which is good. Pain stops you feeling scared.

'You're in for it, now,' I yell into the dazzle. 'Our lawyer's an expert on police brutality. And school brutality.'

I'm not sure about the last bit, but it sounds good. Even though I'm shaking and dizzy, I decide to run for it. I'm a good runner and I reckon I can beat a school caretaker or a sleepy boarding mistress. I stand up.

The torch person grabs my arm.

'Don't try it,' he says.

He's strong. I peer at him through the torch glare. He's not a caretaker or a boarding mistress. I can tell what he is from his clothes.

A bodyguard.

Looks like that boy with the glasses was telling the truth after all.

'Let me go,' I say.

The bodyguard grips my arm harder.

He's about Gavin's age but taller with one of those faces that looks like plasticine.

'This is none of your business,' I say.

'Really?' says the bodyguard, amused at something.

'You're a bodyguard,' I say. 'Your job's stopping people getting in. I'm trying to get out.'

The bodyguard stops smirking. 'Who told you I'm a bodyguard?'

I decide not to dob the kid with glasses in.

'I can tell from that jumper,' I say. 'Only bouncers and bodyguards wear roll-neck jumpers under their jackets.'

The bodyguard looks down at his jumper and frowns.

'My uncle used to work as one,' I say. 'Earlier in his career.'

The bodyguard gives me a strange look. I realise I've almost done it again. Blabbed about my family. I change the subject.

'Why does a kid in this school need a bodyguard?' I ask. 'Does his dad associate with mean and vicious and desperate individuals?'

'None of your business,' says the bodyguard. 'Now go back to bed or I'll report you to the headmaster.'

He lets go of my arm and gives me a little push towards the school buildings.

I decide not to argue. My thoughts are churning faster than a Mongolian dishwasher on pot scrub.

Bodyguards who work all night get paid double time and a half. Only very rich employers can afford to pay that kind of money.

That boy's dad must be a major crime boss. Pity, if I was able to stay at this school, we could have been friends.

## CHAPTER FIVE

I'm taking Gavin's advice.

*Keep to yourself Bridge, and don't nick anything.*

That's what Gavin wrote when he heard I was going to this school. And that's what I've done so far today.

At breakfast, as soon as Ms Hummer stopped trying to introduce me to half the dining hall, I kept to myself. Same in assembly. And now, to get away from all the kids who want to know what it's like to sit on a Melbourne Cup winner, I've come to class early.

I was tempted to say g'day to that boy with the bodyguard, but I didn't. I thought about it, but I reckon Gavin would say the last thing I need right now is being seen hanging around with another crim.

It's peaceful here in the classroom. Nobody around to question me. That's the good thing about being on your own, no risk of giving away family secrets.

I don't know which is my desk, so I sit on the floor up the back.

It's another eight hours till I can see Mum and Dad at parents' night and explain why they have to take me home, so I read Gavin's letter again to keep my spirits up.

*There was a fight at dinner,* he writes. *The kitchen ran out of peas. I kept to myself and kept my nose clean.*

I shouldn't have read that bit. Poor Gavin. I hate to think of him in a place that has random outbreaks of violence and not enough peas.

Thank goodness he's only in there for six months. I hope he manages to keep his nose clean. It's not easy for him because he's allergic to pollen and his sinuses swell up.

A loud noise makes me jump.

The classroom door crashes open.

I stand up.

Two kids come in, both males, average height, thick build, no distinguishing features apart from the sneers on their faces.

'Aw, sookie's reading a letter from Mummy,' says one.

I stuff Gavin's letter into its envelope. Even as I do, I know I'm being dumb. I should be eating it. Too late.

One of the boys lunges towards me and grabs the letter. I hang on to it desperately.

'Come on, give us a read,' says the boy. 'My mummy doesn't write to me.'

'Nor does mine,' says the other boy. He grabs onto the letter too.

I can tell they're both lying.

Most of the scrunched paper is in my hands, but they both have finger-holds on the other end.

I pray the paper doesn't rip. Even if the boys only get a bit of the letter they'll probably see words like *jail* or *six months* or *I wish I never nicked that stuff from those shops* and then the whole school will know the truth about my family.

Other kids have come into the classroom and are standing round watching us struggle.

'Leave her alone, you bullies,' says Antoinette. The boys ignore her.

I'm in a dilemma.

Uncle Ray's a doctor as well as a vet and he's shown me the place on the human body where if you jab it with your fingers the other person goes totally numb for about five minutes. It's illegal, but Uncle Ray reckons it's very effective.

Trouble is, if I do it now, everyone watching will know I've been trained in self-defence by a criminal.

The boy with the bodyguard has just come in and he's hovering, alarmed, eyes as big as Bulgarian chocolate macadamias behind his glasses.

I wish he had his bodyguard here, I could use some help.

It's no good, I can't let these thugs get Gavin's letter. I'll have to numb them and pretend I got how to do it off TV.

I yank on the letter to pull the boys closer into jabbing range. They're not as tough as they look and they stagger forward in surprise and we fall onto the floor in a heap.

For a second I can't hear anything. Then I get my head out from under a leg just as a teacher's voice roars from the doorway.

'What is going on?'

It's Mr Lamb, our class teacher. The headmaster told Mum and Dad that Mr Lamb used to play rugby for Wales, and I can see he's still got the red face you get in scrums.

He's glaring at me and the boys, who are scrambling to their feet. I wish Mr Creely was here with his gameboy to keep a friendly eye on me and protect me. Now Mr Lamb is glaring at the letter crumpled in my hand.

'What is that document?' he says. 'The one that seems to be causing so much trouble?'

My guts turn to the sort of mush you usually only find in Latvian bread-making machines.

The bodyguard boy darts across and bends over me. Before I can gather my thoughts he pulls Gavin's letter out of my hand.

I sit up to jab him.

Before I can, he does an amazing thing.

Still bending over me, keeping his back to Mr Lamb and the other kids, the bodyguard boy stuffs Gavin's letter into my blazer pocket. From his own pocket he takes another envelope.

He turns and hands his envelope to Mr Lamb. 'It's some sort of letter, sir,' he says.

'Thank you, Menzies,' says Mr Lamb.

'Dobber,' hisses Chantelle.

But I'm thinking this kid called Menzies isn't a dobber. I reckon he knows I'm in the same boat as him, but without a bodyguard.

He's trying to help me.

While Mr Lamb pulls the letter out of the envelope and studies it, I wonder if this is the letter Menzies was reading yesterday and getting upset over.

Mr Lamb starts reading out loud.

*'Today the man in the next cell yelled the names of his children and then tried to climb over the razor wire fence. Some other prisoners stopped him but he still hurt himself. I explained to the guards that the man just needed to know when he was going to get out. "Don't ask me," said one of the guards. "I can't see that far into the future." He laughed. I had to stop Bibi from biting him on the ankle.'*

Mr Lamb rolls his eyes, folds up the letter and puts it back into the envelope.

I'm feeling sick.

This is terrible.

This is no help at all.

Menzies' letter is from someone in a maximum security jail. No wonder Menzies was upset if it's a brother or a cousin or an uncle. I'm upset, too. Now everyone will think I've got a murderer in the family.

Before I can get my letter out and show everyone that Gavin's just a harmless shoplifter, Mr Lamb gives a big sigh and points to me with Menzies' letter.

'It seems we have another refugee sympathiser among us,' says Mr Lamb. 'Did Menzies arrange this penfriend for you?'

Refugee sympathiser? Penfriend? I don't understand. I don't know what to say.

'Menzies needs to learn that not everybody is as obsessed as he is about refugees in detention centres,' Mr Lamb goes on. 'I'm beginning to wonder if that refugee project I set last term was a mistake.'

He holds the letter out to me.

He obviously wants me to take it.

I take it.

'There's only one type of detention I'm interested in right now,' says Mr Lamb, glaring at me and the two bully boys. 'And that's the detention the three of you will be doing at lunchtime.'

The class take their seats and Mr Lamb shows me where my desk is. As I realise what's happened, the sick feeling goes. I give Menzies a grateful look across the classroom.

He has helped me.

A lot.

These people don't think I'm part of a major crime family, they just think I'm a refugee sympathiser.

Perhaps, just perhaps, I can stay at this school after all.

## CHAPTER SIX

I knock urgently on Menzies' door.

Lunchtime's almost over, but I want to thank him for helping me. I also want to ask him how I can get a refugee penfriend like his.

It's a brilliant way of keeping his crim family secret. If ever he forgets himself and blabs about prisoners or cells or visiting hours, people just think he's talking about a detention centre.

Perhaps it'll work for me too.

I knock again.

Come on, Menzies. If I'm sprung here in the boys' building I'll be back in detention myself.

Someone taps me on the shoulder. Startled, I turn round.

And freeze.

It's the bodyguard.

I recognise him instantly, even though in daylight his face doesn't look so much like plasticine. And instead of a black roll-neck jumper he's wearing a Britney Spears t-shirt. I can tell he recognises me from the way he takes a bite of his toast and chews it slowly without taking his eyes off me.

Now I'm in for it. Unlike last night, this is definitely his business. It's his job, apprehending intruders like me and keeping them away from his client. Specially female ones who aren't even meant to be in the building.

'Hello,' says the bodyguard, flicking crumbs off his t-shirt. 'I see you've decided to postpone your departure.'

I don't get it. He's not apprehending me. He's not even telling me to get out of the boys' building. Perhaps he doesn't know about the rule.

'I'm looking for Menzies,' I say.

'He's in there,' says the bodyguard, nodding towards Menzies' room. 'Don't bother knocking, he won't hear you. Just go in.'

The bodyguard strolls off down the corridor.

I'm shocked. He's not even trying to protect his client. Just wandering around the school making toast. This is pathetic. Menzies' dad is being ripped off. It's criminal.

I step inside, wondering what the bodyguard meant about Menzies not hearing me.

The room looks empty. Then I hear muffled sounds coming from the wardrobe.

Uncle Grub, who used to do a lot of burglary when he was first married, reckons the minute you first step into a room you can tell if something's wrong.

There's definitely something wrong in this room.

I wish the door hadn't swung shut behind me.

The muffled sounds in the wardrobe

are getting louder.

I try to think what might be making them.

Noisy hot water pipes? A guard dog that Menzies keeps hidden in the wardrobe? Menzies in some kind of trouble?

I pull the wardrobe door open and get ready to dive behind the bed if it's a fierce dog.

It's not.

It's Menzies, in a lot of trouble.

He's handcuffed to the clothes rail and his ankles are tied together with a towel and he has a pair of underpants stuffed in his mouth. He's glaring at me through his big round glasses. He looks cross and upset and embarrassed.

I pull the underpants out of his mouth. 'Thanks,' he mutters.

'Are you OK?' I ask.

He nods, but I can see he didn't like the taste of the underpants.

'What happened?' I say.

'Nothing,' he says.

I understand. He's trying to protect his family's identity. Probably a kidnap attempt or some sort of gangland

42

revenge.

'I reckon it's really unfair,' I say. 'People shouldn't have to suffer because of what their parents do.'

Menzies doesn't agree or disagree. He just tells me that the key for the handcuffs is on the bedside table.

I find the key and unlock the cuffs.

Menzies falls out of the wardrobe onto the carpet. I realise I should have untied his ankles first.

'Whose handcuffs are they?' I ask as I unknot the towel.

'Dave's,' says Menzies crossly. 'My bodyguard.'

I stare at him.

'Your own bodyguard did this?'

I try to make sense of it. Perhaps Menzies was so desperate to have lunch with the other kids in the dining hall that the dopey bodyguard had to restrain him. Or perhaps it's some sort of training exercise.

'Dave lent me his handcuffs for a school project,' says Menzies.

He sits on the bed and rubs his wrists and ankles.

'Then who did it?' I say.

Menzies suddenly looks sad and I can see he's going to tell me the truth.

'Kids from class,' he says. 'They thought I was being a dobber with the letter. Plus they blamed me for Rich and Trav getting detention.'

'That's not fair,' I explode. 'You were just helping me.'

Menzies picks his lunch tray up off the floor. Stuck to it is an empty yoghurt pot.

'It was six against one,' he says. 'But they didn't get it all their own way. I stuffed yoghurt in Bryce Wentworth's mouth. He hates yoghurt.'

'Good on you,' I say. 'I wish I'd been here to help.'

Menzies looks at me sadly and nods. He has a big splodge of yoghurt in his hair. I try not to stare at it. Instead I pull his letter out of my pocket and hold it out to him.

'Thanks for what you did,' I say. 'It was really kind.'

Menzies takes the letter. 'I could see you wanted to keep your letter private,' he says.

I want to say more. I want to tell him

how much we've got in common. How if I stay at the school we can be friends and allies and look out for each other.

But first there's something I have to ask.

'The kids who did this, why didn't your bodyguard stop them?'

I think I already know the answer. Because he was off making toast.

Menzies sighs. 'Dave doesn't interfere with school stuff. He's just here to guard me from bigger stuff. You know, terrorists.'

I stare at him.

Terrorists? Menzies' family is in danger from terrorists.'

Suddenly Dad's Bulgarian associates don't seem so bad.

'Look,' I say, 'I don't want to pry, but my dad might be able to give your dad some advice about how to get on with difficult business partners. For example my dad's discovered it's a big mistake to ask for a receipt.'

Menzies is looking at me like he doesn't have a clue what I'm talking about.

'My father's a minister,' he says.

Now it's my turn to be confused. Why would terrorists want to harm the son of a minister? Perhaps his dad was rude about them in a sermon.

'What religion?' I ask.

'Not that sort of minister,' says Menzies. 'A government minister. My father's the Minister for National Development. He criticised a terrorist organisation, so now I have to have a bodyguard.'

'Oh,' I say.

I let all this sink in.

'I see,' I add after a while.

What I see mostly is how tragic it is. For the first time ever I almost had a real friend. A lonely crim kid just like me, but brave and clever too.

Now I'm just glad I didn't blab any more details to him about Mum, Dad or Bulgarian exporters.

'Oh no,' groans Menzies, feeling in his blazer pocket. 'They put jam in my pockets.'

Poor kid. I do feel sorry for him. The other kids probably think he's up himself because his dad's more important than their dads.

But I can't do anything about that.

What I have to concentrate on is getting as far away from Menzies as I can. Before he finds out any more about my family and suddenly the police and customs and the Department of Overseas Trade are busting into our place with search warrants.

I feel sick and shaky. I just want to be at home in my own bed.

I'm so glad parents' night is tonight so I can tell Mum and Dad how desperately I need to get out of this place.


## CHAPTER SEVEN


I wish this school didn't have a parents' night.

It's a disaster.

Parents' night is on the first evening of term so all the country parents can come before they head back home, and the trouble with country people is they're really chatty.

'How's it going?' Antoinette's mum just asked Dad. 'Making a crust?'

I'm sure half the school hall heard Dad telling her how last month's heavy rain in Turkmenistan was great for business. I tried to distract him, but he just went on about the seriously top-notch mudslides and how a lot of Russian trucks got bogged and how his business partners own the only tow truck for two thousand square kilometres. If he tells everyone how the going rate for a tow in those parts is thirty washing machines or sixty dryers, we're history.

Mum's usually good at keeping a cork in Dad, but she's being distracted by Antoinette who's telling her about Brad's brave battle with hoof mould.

I've got to get Mum and Dad outside for an urgent talk. The only reason I'm not doing it now is they sent me off to get them a drink.

I'm hurrying back with two glasses of fruit punch.

Oh no. Now Dad's talking to Veuve's parents. I heard Veuve boasting this afternoon how her parents are in the

48

media. They could be recording everything Dad's saying.

There's only one thing to do.

Pretend to trip.

'Sorry, Dad,' I say.

Two glasses of fruit punch fly through the air. 'Ow, Bridget, what are you doing?' wails Dad. 'I'm soaked.'

Fruit punch drips off his suit. Luckily it's one of the Lebanese ones that arrived last week so he's got another hundred and seventy.

'Get cold water on it,' say Antoinette's parents.

'And salt,' say Veuve's parents.

'Come on: I say to Mum and Dad. 'The toilets are outside. We'll grab a bowl of peanuts on the way.'

I drag them out of the hall with Mum dabbing at Dad's front with a tissue. In the courtyard I turn and face them both.

'I'm sorry, Dad,' I say. 'I'm sorry, Mum. This is a nightmare.'

'No it's not, love,' says Mum gently. 'It was an accident. We all have accidents sometimes. Remember when Dad tried to wash nine thousand pairs of pearl earrings in the dishwasher and they melted?'

'I don't mean spilling the punch,' I say. 'I mean this school. Look at the other kids. Look at their parents. I shouldn't be here.'

I hold my breath.

Mum and Dad look at each other, and then back at me.

'I know what you're saying, love,' says Dad. I nod, heart racing. Good old Dad.

'That bloke I was just talking to who produces TV game shows,' continues Dad. 'He reckons he uses fake gold watches for his prizes and charges the network for real ones. And the woman who owns the cosmetics factory. She makes that soap that's meant to get rid of wrinkles and she just told me it doesn't. OK, sometimes in this world we have to bend the rules to make a crust, but that's no excuse for lying and cheating.'

'Len,' says Mum. 'I don't think that's what Bridget means.'

Dad frowns.

'This school is too dangerous,' I say.

'There are kids here whose parents are judges. And commissioners of police. And cosmetics manufacturers who can make citizens' arrests if they want to. If they find out what we do, we're in big trouble.'

Dad looks at me, still frowning.

'What do you mean,' he says, 'what we do?'

He's making me say it and I wish I didn't have to. 'What you do,' I say quietly.

Dad's puzzled frown turns into a sad and hurt one.

Mum puts her arms round me.

'Love,' she says. 'I think you're worrying too much.'

'No,' says Dad quietly. 'I know what you're saying, Bridget.'

This time I can see he really does.

'Which is why,' continues Dad, 'I want you to stay at this school. In years to come, when you tell people you went here, and about the friends you made here, doors will open. You can do great things. Have any career you want. No need for secrets. No need to be ashamed.'

I look Dad in the eyes, which is hard because mine are filling with tears.

'I'm not ashamed now, Dad,' I say.

Dad nods, but his eyes aren't meeting mine any more.

'This is a good school,' says Mum. 'With a wonderful academic record. And I'm sure the people here are too busy with their own lives to worry about us.'

Dad puts his arms round me and Mum.

'I know it's not easy for you here, Bridget,' he says. 'But we Whites don't give up, eh? Your great-great-great grandfather Benedict White didn't give up. He was arrested in 1847 for leading a shearers' strike and he tunnelled his way out of the police stockade using just his bare hands.'

I hate that.

Whenever Dad wants me to do something yuk, he brings up great-great-great grandad White, which wasn't even his real name. We changed it when we changed ours.

I wish Benedict White had got locked up in 1847 and stayed locked up.

Mum is looking at me, concerned.

'Poor love,' she says. 'Must still be a bit strange and lonely here.'

I shrug. If I'm staying at this school, no point in worrying them further.

'Hang in there,' says Dad. He taps me fondly on the chin with his fist. 'In four days you'll be home for the weekend. Very important event this Saturday. I hope you haven't forgotten.'

'Your birthday,' I say, trying to sound enthusiastic rather than hopeless.

'And all I want for my birthday,' says Dad, 'is a happy daughter.'

'Give her time,' says Mum, stroking my hair. 'You'll feel much better, love, once you've made your first friend. Those girls with the horses seem lovely.'

'Hello, Bridget,' says a voice.

I turn and my insides droop like a soggy pearl earring.

It's Menzies, blinking through his glasses. He looks sort of hopeful and sad at the same time.

I try to think of a way to get rid of

him without hurting his feelings.

'Can I hang out with you for a bit?' says Menzies. 'My parents haven't turned up.'

'Oh, you poor thing,' says Mum. 'Of course you can. Bridget, come on love, introduce your friend.'

'This is Menzies,' I mumble.

'Pleased to meet you, Menzies,' say Mum and Dad, looking even more pleased than when they last heard it was raining in Turkmenistan.

I look around for the bodyguard but I can't see him. He must be getting himself some punch. Or toast.

'My parents were going to be here,' says Menzies, 'but they're very busy.'

'That's bad luck,' says Dad. 'What do they do?'

'My father's the Minister for National Development,' says Menzies. 'My mother helps him with policy and entertaining.'

Mum and Dad don't say anything for ages. Just give each other delighted glances. I stare at the damp patch on Dad's suit and wonder if Menzies would be scared off if I tell him that

Dad's got a bladder problem.

Before I can work out how to do to it without Dad hearing, Mum remembers how to speak.

'Well, Menzies,' she says, 'we're very glad our daughter's got you for a friend.'

'That's right,' says Dad. 'It's my birthday on Saturday. We're having a bit of a family celebration at our place and Bridget's coming home for the weekend. We'd be delighted if you could come with her.'

'Yes,' says Mum. 'Delighted.'

I stare at them both in horror.

Menzies' eyes are shining behind his glasses. 'Thank you,' he says to Mum and Dad. 'That's very kind. I'd like to very much.'

'You can't,' I croak.

All three of them look at me.

'It's too dangerous,' I say to Menzies. 'The terrorist warnings, remember? Your bodyguard won't let you.'

Menzies smiles at me and I can see he's feeling touched.

'It's OK,' he says. 'I'll get permission from my parents. They won't mind. I'm sure there are no terrorists at your place.'


## CHAPTER EIGHT

I snap awake.

Dream voices are spinning round inside my head like bits of a Mongolian electric toothbrush when it disintegrates in your mouth.

Dad telling Veuve's dad he's a disgrace to the school.

Me begging Menzies not to come to my place on Saturday.

Uncle Grub explaining the features of a Russian blender.

Hang on, that last one isn't part of a dream. I'm wide awake now and I can hear Uncle Grub's voice echoing around the courtyard outside.

Oh no.

I struggle out of my tangle of sheets, clamber onto Chantelle's bed, drag the curtains open and stick my head out the window.

'Ow,' moans Chantelle. 'You're

standing on my stomach.'

I know how she feels. My guts are hurting too. In my case it's because of what I'm looking at.

Uncle Grub's black Hi-Ace van is parked by the side door of the dining hall. Uncle Grub is deep in conversation with Dave the bodyguard. They're both examining a blender.

'Really strong blades,' Uncle Grub is saying. 'Made for turnips and beetroot and all that other Russian stuff.'

I leap off Chantelle's stomach and start dragging on clothes. The three girls peer sleepily out of the window.

'Oh yuk', says Veuve. 'Look at the greasy pony-tail on that delivery man.'

I fling myself down the stairs and sprint across the courtyard towards the van. Dave the bodyguard is strolling off towards his room with a blender under his arm. I pray he doesn't decide to check whether import duty's been paid on it.

So far nobody else is around.

'Uncle Grub,' I hiss. 'What are you doing here?'

Uncle Grub emerges from the back

of the van, a big grin on his face.

'G'day, gorgeous,' he says. 'How's posh school?'

He kisses me on the head and the scent of his Bosnian aftershave reminds me of so many happy family afternoons in the back yard, with table tennis and Bulgarian chocolate biscuits, that for a moment I forget him being here could ruin us all.

Then I remember.

It's not safe,' I hiss.

'Relax, darl,' says Uncle Grub. 'Just got a little delivery for you. Your dad had the idea driving home from here last night. He's at the docks this morning, so he asked me to do it.'

I can't relax. My guts feel like Chantelle, Antoinette and Veuve are all jumping on them, along with Gandalf, Brad and Muffy.

The van is stacked to the roof with Russian blenders. Uncle Grub pulls one out of its box, takes it out of its plastic bag and inspects it closely.

'That's the one thing with Russian blenders,' he says. 'Got to check them for rust.'

'What do you mean, a delivery for me?' I croak.

'To help you settle in,' says Uncle Grub. 'Little gift for the teachers. They'll all love you once they see how these things chop turnips.'

Around our feet are empty blender boxes and plastic bags. The van is backed up to the open side door of the dining hall. I peer in. At the far end of the hall is the top table where the teachers have their breakfast. No teachers are there yet, but next to each empty cereal bowl stands a Russian blender.

'Quick,' I say to Uncle Grub. 'We've got about five minutes before the teachers start arriving.'

'What's the matter?' says Uncle Grub, concerned. 'Did I miss a rusty one?'

Before I can rush into the dining hall and start grabbing blenders, a voice rings out across the courtyard.

'Miss White, a moment please.'

Striding towards us, head cocked quizzically, is Mr Galbraith. I can see he's wondering who Uncle Grub is.

'It's the headmaster,' I hiss at Uncle Grub.

'G'day chief,' says Uncle Grub, stepping forward and shaking Mr Galbraith's hand. 'Sorry about the early visit. George White, Bridget's uncle.'

Uncle Grub holds a Russian blender out to Mr Galbraith.

'On behalf of the White family,' says Uncle Grub, 'we hope you'll accept this quality appliance. A little expression of our gratitude for the good care you're taking of Bridget, and a symbol of her desire to blend in happily with the students and staff at this fine school.'

Mr Galbraith stares at the blender. Then, slowly, he takes it.

'Thank you,' he says. 'This is a bit irregular, but a very nice thought. I'll donate it to the school kitchen. Glad to see you're settling in well, Bridget. Good to meet you, Mr White. Goodbye now.'

Mr Galbraith strolls away across the courtyard, examining the blender.

'See,' says Uncle Grub, grinning at me. 'Nothing smooths a path through life like a Russian blender.'

I glance anxiously into the dining hall. Teachers are starting to arrive now, picking up their blenders and staring at them. Kids are arriving too, staring at the teachers.

Uncle Grub is picking up the empty boxes and plastic bags and chucking them into the back of the van.

'Can't be too careful,' he says. 'Plastic bags can be dangerous when there are kiddies around.'

So can uncles, I think miserably.

'Got to be getting back,' says Uncle Grub, closing the doors of the van. 'Bloke coming round with an automatic teller machine he needs some help with.' He kisses me on the head and murmurs into my ear. 'You don't have to feel ashamed of your family here, Bridget. Compared to some of the families at this place, we're angels.'

'I know,' I say.

Uncle Grub gets into the van. 'See you at the weekend,' he says. 'Be good.'

He drives off and the dust from his wheels swirls around me. Inside me, sad feelings do the same.

I'll never be ashamed of my family. Dad is a top-notch angel, trying to make things better for me here. But that doesn't stop me worrying. The people at this school are already getting suspicious about us. The dining hall's full of teachers and kids talking about the blenders and giving me strange looks. I can't let any more information about us leak out.

That's why I have to tell Menzies he can't come to Dad's birthday party.


## CHAPTER NINE

I hurry along the corridor to Menzies' room.

In my head I rehearse what I'm going to say to him. How Mum and Dad have been called away to Turkmenistan on business. How the birthday party's been cancelled. How I'm only going home on the weekend to feed the goldfish.

Look at me. I've only been at this school for three days and I'm lying already.

I hate doing it but I have to.

As I pass the room next to Menzies', I hear the sound of a Russian blender going at full speed. No teachers live on this floor, so it must be Dave the bodyguard's room. I hope he's holding the lid on tight. That's another thing about Russian blenders. Loose lids.

I knock on Menzies' door.

After a bit he opens it.

'Hello,' he says, glaring at me.

I'm confused. Does Menzies know what I'm about to say? How can he?

'Come in,' he says crossly.

For a moment I wonder if the kids from class have been back. But when I step into the room I see a breakfast tray that hasn't been touched, and next to it an envelope, torn open.

Menzies is holding a crumpled sheet of paper.

'What's wrong?' I say.

'I've had another letter,' he says.

'From the refugee detention centre?' I say.

He stops, giving me a quick glare.

'You probably think it's all stupid,'

he says. 'Like everyone else around here.'

'No,' I say quietly. 'I don't.'

For a second I'm tempted to tell him some of my feelings about jails. You spend a lot of time thinking about them when your brother's in one. But I decide not to risk it.

Menzies looks pale and tense. He doesn't look like someone who's writing to the refugees to get something out of it for himself. He looks like someone who's so upset about them that he's not even eating properly.

'Why don't you have some breakfast?' I say.

Dad reckons everything in the world seems worse without breakfast.

I take a piece of toast from Menzies' breakfast tray and offer it to him. He grabs it and chucks it across the room. Either he hates toast or he's very angry.

'It's not fair,' he says. 'The refugees haven't done anything wrong. They shouldn't be locked up. It's not like they're thieves or criminals.'

I don't know what to say.

'Listen to this,' says Menzies. He smooths out the letter and reads.

*'The Australian government say we are queue jumpers, but it's not true. In Afghanistan everyone made queues except the people who were shot. In this detention centre we also queue. For soap, for food, for water. People with headaches have to queue for pills. But we don't complain because if we do the guards shout at us and that's not good for the people with headaches.'*

'That's awful,' I say.

It is. Even Gavin doesn't have to queue for aspirin. When he has a headache he just bangs on his cell door and yells and a guard brings him some.

Menzies reads more.

*'I am sorry if I get some of these words wrong, Menzies. The kind person here who helps me write this letter in English is very sad. His wife and two daughters drowned on the boat trip to Australia. Sometimes his tears fall on the letter. He says sorry about the wet marks.'*

Menzies' voice gives a wobble. He stops reading and glares at his porridge. I don't want him to see I've noticed the wobble in case he feels embarrassed, so I say something quickly.

'Is he the same man who sent you the other letter, the one you had in class yesterday?'

Menzies nods.

I wonder why a detention centre has to be even worse than a jail.

'Except,' says Menzies, 'he's not a man, he's a kid.'

I stare at him. I thought I was shocked before, but now I'm really shocked.

'A kid?' I say.

'His name's Jamal,' says Menzies. 'He's the same age as us.'

'But that's impossible,' I say. 'Kids don't get locked up.'

'There are lots of them in the detention centres,' says Menzies. 'Jamal's got a younger sister, Bibi. She's had toothache on and off for the last month.'

My head is spinning.

Menzies reads more of Jamal's letter.

*'The people who run this detention*

*centre don't give the guards a present on their birthdays. No wonder the guards are often bitter and cross. So me and Bibi are making presents for them. I'm making soccer balls out of plastic bags and string from my blanket. Bibi is making little mountain lions out of dry grass and dirt and spit. We hope this will give us a happier detention centre and cheer Mum and Dad up. They are very sad because the Australian government won't tell us how long our prison sentence is.'*

Menzies stops again.

This time I'm the one who can't speak.

I'm thinking about something Gavin has said to me a few times. How the one thing that helps him get through his prison sentence is counting the days. Knowing exactly how much time he's got left.

Imagine not knowing when you're going to be free.

Imagine not knowing if you ever are.

Jamal's right, that's not fair.

'What did they do?' I ask. 'To get locked up like that?'

67

Menzies goes to his desk, pulls a bundle of letters out of the drawer and holds them out to me. 'The government in Afghanistan tried to kill them. Blew up their house.'

I give a whistle.

Even the police special branch wouldn't do that here.

I don't take the letters from Menzies. Best to not get involved. But there's something I have to ask.

'Why did the government blow up their house?' I say. 'Are the family really big criminals?'

Menzies shakes his head. 'Jamal and Bibi's parents ran a school in their home.'

I can't believe it. The death penalty just for running a school. Gavin stole a really expensive cuckoo clock and confessed to fifty-three similar offenses and he only got six months.

'The family escaped from Afghanistan,' says Menzies. 'They wanted to get as far away as they could, so they tried to come to Australia. The Australian government put them in a detention centre, first on an island somewhere, then in the desert here.'

Suddenly I don't want to hear any more.

Suddenly the whole thing's making me feel ill.

The one thought that's kept me going all these years, the piece of good news I tell myself every time I lie awake worrying about Mum and Dad's profession, is that kids don't get locked up. So if Mum and Dad ever have to go to jail, I can stay outside and look after things. Take care of the house and pets, plus visit Mum and Dad with cakes.

'It must be a mistake,' I say. 'The government must have got the paperwork wrong. Your dad's a government minister. Can't he do something? Get the kids parole or something?'

Menzies gives a big sigh.

'I try,' he says. 'I ask him but we just end up arguing. He says I'm too young to understand. I tell him a three year old knows you shouldn't lock innocent kids up. My mother butts in and tells me not to speak to my father like that.

69

It's really hard trying to get them to listen over the phone.'

'Why don't you speak to him in person?' I say.

'When?' demands Menzies, getting cross again.

'It was the holidays four days ago,' I say, puzzled. 'Why didn't you ask him then?'

Menzies doesn't reply, and I wonder if he's got secrets about his family after all. Or if eating porridge for breakfast makes you a bit slow.

Then he does reply. 'I didn't actually see my parents these holidays,' he says. 'They were overseas on a trade mission.'

He looks so sad I want to put my arms round him. I don't because this is the boys' building and I'm not even meant to be here.

'What did you do?' I ask. 'Stay here?'

'Don't be an idiot,' says Menzies. 'Who'd want to be at school in the holidays? I stayed with my uncle and aunt on their farm. They don't like me much. We argue a lot. They think refugee boats should be sunk. For the last few days Dave went to visit his mum in Canberra. I had to come back to school in a police car.'

I try to imagine what it would be like, not seeing your mum and dad in the holidays. Just mean rellies and a public servant who's trained to kill.

Compared to Menzies I'm lucky. I've got Mum and Dad.

'It's not my parents' fault,' says Menzies. 'They do very important work for Australia. I'm proud of them.'

I look closely to see if he really is.

He's not looking at me any more, he's staring at his porridge again.

'But I wish they had a bit more free time,' he says.

He's trying to hide it, but I can see his eyes behind his big glasses. I can see how wistful they are.

Suddenly I know I can't do it.

I can't lie.

It'll be a huge risk, but we'll survive somehow.

'My parents really like you, Menzies,' I say. 'They're really looking forward to seeing you at the party on Saturday.'

# CHAPTER TEN

'Take that, you lousy cop,' yells Dad.

He rolls out from behind the coffee table, aims his gun at Dave the bodyguard, and fires.

'No,' screams Mum.

Dad's shot misses.

I take cover. So does everyone else in the room.

Dave dives behind the couch, firing back.

His shot hits Dad in the head.

Dad groans and slumps back against the coffee table. I fling myself across the room towards him, but it's too late. A beer bottle on the coffee table topples onto the carpet. Luckily it's empty.

'Ow,' says Dad, rubbing his head. 'That hurts.'

Most of us laugh because he does look funny with a small plastic arrow stuck to his forehead.

'You nearly knocked the drinks over,' says Mum.

'Sorry,' says Dad.

My cousins, who are all under six, stare anxiously at Dad's head. Uncle Ollie, who used to be a male nurse before he was a baggage handler, is staring at it too.

'So, Dave,' he says. 'Is that where you guys are trained to put the first shot?'

Dave, picking himself up from behind the couch, rolls his eyes. 'Fair go. I'm on duty. We agreed no personal questions, right?'

'That's right,' says Dad, giving Uncle Ollie a look. He yanks the plastic arrow off his head. The rubber tip makes a loud pop.

We all laugh again, Dad and the little cousins included.

I'm laughing loudest because I'm so nervous. A federal policeman in our house. One mistake and we'll be having Dad's birthday party next year in the clink.

So far so good, though. Dad had a word to everyone about watching what they say. Even Uncle Grub hasn't put his foot in it yet, though I personally think giving Dad plastic cowboy guns for his birthday was a bit careless.

'Hey, George,' says Dad, waving the plastic arrow at Uncle Grub. 'I thought these things were meant to be harmless.'

'Don't blame me, Len,' says Uncle Grub, grinning. 'They're from your warehouse.'

Everyone laughs again, except me.

I can't believe it. Uncle Grub mentioned the warehouse.

Luckily Dave is more concerned with picking carpet fluff off his roll-neck sweater. Before he can ask what else is in the warehouse and does Dad have import papers for it all, I zoom in with a plate of little puff pastries filled with prawns. Soon Dave is munching happily and chatting to Mum.

I stand next to Mum with the plate. She doesn't like prawns but I want to keep an ear on what they're saying. Mum's been looking a bit emotional today. I think it's because Gavin can't be here for Dad's birthday.

'Good party, Mrs W,' says Dave.

'Call me Roz,' says Mum. 'It's a

pleasure having you and Menzies here. Next time we hope Menzies' parents can come too.'

Dave stops chewing. 'Dunno about that,' he says, looking doubtful.

'Perhaps Menzies can ask them,' suggests Mum.

Dave frowns. 'His dad's pretty busy. His mum's the one who does most of the parenting. Still, I always reckon a bloke's pretty lucky if he's got his mum there for him.'

I realise Mum is biting her lip, struggling to control her feelings. She's thinking about Gavin.

I thrust the plate of pastries at Dave again to distract him.

Uncle Ollie's wife Del swoops in and steers Mum out into the garden. Dave watches Mum go, frowning. I dig him in the stomach with the plate.

'Would you like another vol-au-vent?' I ask.

It's a word I learned from Antoinette in home economics.

Instead of answering, Dave suddenly looks around.

'Where's Menzies?' he says.

With a jolt of alarm I realise Menzies isn't in the room. The guest of honour has wandered off.

'I saw him go upstairs,' says Uncle Ray.

'Probably having a pee,' says Uncle Ray's wife Bernie.

'I'll find him,' I say. I dump the plate of pastries in Dave's hands so cocktail sauce splashes onto his shirt, and while he's brushing himself off I leap up the stairs.

The last thing we want is a Federal cop wandering around upstairs. It's bad enough having Menzies up here. Last time I looked there were Iraqi pressure cookers stacked in Gavin's room and US army electric toothbrushes under Mum and Dad's bed. I think there might be US army toothpaste in the bathroom cabinet, too.

I tap urgently on the bathroom door.

'Menzies,' I hiss.

That kid can be a real pain sometimes. Dad was very clear about everyone using the downstairs dunny.

No answer. I open the bathroom door. Menzies isn't in there.

'Menzies,' I hiss louder.

If he's poking around under Mum and Dad's bed, I'll have to hit him with a pressure cooker and hope concussion makes him forget what he's seen.

OK, I wouldn't really do that. Dad hates violence even more than swearing.

Suddenly I hear Menzies' voice, loud and heated, coming from my room. I hurry in. Menzies is sitting on the floor, shouting into his mobile phone.

'You just don't care, do you? You don't care that innocent kids are suffering. Well you can tell Dad that when I'm eighteen I'm not voting for him. Ever.'

He snaps the phone shut and throws it across the floor. He slumps back against my bed. Then he realises I'm in the room. He looks up at me, eyes big and angry behind his glasses.

Suddenly I feel angry too.

'If you wanted to spend the weekend talking to your parents,' I say, 'why did you come here?'

And put me under so much stress, I want to add. So I'm probably going to need blood pressure tablets by the time I'm thirty, like Uncle Ollie.

I don't say that. Menzies mustn't know there's any reason for me to be stressed. I try to stop glaring at him.

'I've had another letter from Jamal,' says Menzies quietly. 'Things are getting worse.'

'What do you mean?' I ask.

'The guards at the detention centre won't believe Bibi gets toothache; he says. 'A dentist looked at her when her tooth wasn't hurting and he said she was making it up.'

'Didn't the x-ray show the problem?' I ask.

'They don't have x-rays in detention centres,' says Menzies. 'You have to be taken to hospital for that. Jamal's got a plan to get Bibi taken there.'

I find myself hoping it's not anything dangerous.

'A soccer match,' says Menzies. 'And if that doesn't work, a hunger strike.'

It's worse than I'd imagined.

'You know what a hunger strike is,' says Menzies.

'It's where people refuse to eat

anything.'

'I know what a hunger strike is,' I say.

I tried it once with Mum when I was about three. She just held my nose and shoved the food into my mouth. They don't do that with bigger people. They do something much worse. One of the prisoners in Gavin's section went on a hunger strike and Gavin told me what happened to the poor bloke.

'A hunger strike's not a good idea,' I say.

'I know,' says Menzies, his face pale with concern. 'You can get malnutrition. You can even die.'

Poor Menzies looks so upset I don't tell him what else can happen.


## CHAPTER ELEVEN

I grab Menzies' phone off my bedroom floor.

'Ring Jamal,' I say. 'Try and persuade him not to do the hunger strike.'

Menzies shakes his head.

'Send him an email then,' I say.

'People in his detention centre are only allowed to get letters,' Menzies says. 'It's Sunday so I can't write to him till tomorrow.'

We look at each other gloomily.

Menzies gives me the new letter from Jamal, then goes downstairs to show Dave he hasn't been kidnapped by terrorists or by voters who want Sunday mail collections.

I lock myself in the bathroom and read.

*Dear Menzies,*

*Me and Bibi gave one of the guards his birthday presents yesterday. A soccer ball and a desert lion.*

*'Happy Birthday, sir,' we said.*

*'Thanks 5603 and 5604,' said the guard.*

*I wish he hadn't said that. Bibi hates being called by her number. She snatched the desert lion back and threw it into the guard's coffee. We had to spend the rest of the day in our room. I could smell the soccer ball burning in the incinerator.*

*I'm not giving up.*

*Sir Alex Ferguson, the manager of Manchester United, said the secret of soccer is to never give up even if things are looking hopeless. I think that's also the secret of surviving in a detention centre.*

*I've got a new idea.*

*I'm arranging a soccer match between the refugees and the guards. Soccer is a good way to make friends and cheer people up, even parents who are getting very depressed.*

*There are some problems. My hip is still very sore where a pirate kicked it on our journey to Australia. Several of the other soccer players here are injured also, or have insomnia. Plus some of the guards hate soccer and make fun of us when we play. I think they'll change their mind once they play it.*

*I hope so because Bibi often has toothache but the guards do not believe her. The dentist could not find the pain and stopped looking when Bibi called him a camel snot.*

*She needs an x-ray in hospital.*

*I think the guards will agree after*

*they've played soccer with her.*

*But in case they don't, I also have another plan. A hunger plan. I have seen people in this detention centre stop eating food for many days or even weeks, and after that time they are taken to hospital.*

*If we must, me and Bibi will stop eating food. I will too because you can't ask your younger sister to stop eating food if you don't. After a number of days or weeks the Australian government will know that Bibi really has toothache because who would stop eating food if they or their sister didn't really have toothache?*

*I hope we don't have to do this. I know hunger will hurt a lot but we will survive because our ancestors were bakers and desert warriors and they were very tough. Also we feel strong because you are our friend, Menzies.*

*I hope your family are well and safe. What is your father's job? My father is a taxi driver, but now he queues with my mother for food for me and Bibi. (You know what parents are like.) He also writes many letters to the National Library trying to learn about Australian*

*law to get us out of here.*
  *Your friend,*
  *Jamal*

## CHAPTER TWELVE

I lie in my bed, staring into the darkness. Downstairs in the living room the Bulgarian cuckoo clock strikes midnight.

I wish I could stay here for ever, snuggled safe and warm under the covers, my tummy full of Mum's apple and chocolate biscuit crumble, my lips tingling with Dad's US army toothpaste.

But I can't.

There's something I have to do.

'Menzies,' I whisper. 'Are you awake?'

'Yes,' he whispers from the mattress on the floor.

I knew he would be. When everyone finally went home, yawning and saying what a good party it had been, and Mum and Dad started yawning too,

Menzies and I just looked at each other.

How can people sleep, Menzies' look said, when kids are suffering injustice?

I lean out of bed so I can whisper to Menzies very quietly. You can't be too careful when there's a federal policeman asleep on the couch in the living room.

'I've been thinking,' I whisper. 'If I ask your dad to help Jamal and Bibi, perhaps he'll listen to me. I'm not related to him so he won't feel like his kid's trying to boss him around.'

In the green glow from my Albanian alarm clock, I can see Menzies thinking about this. I don't tell him exactly what I'm going to say to his dad, the gory details, because I don't want to upset him.

'You'll have to make sure you don't lose your temper,' says Menzies. 'He can be really stubborn.'

'It's OK,' I say. 'Some of my family are a bit pig-headed too.'

Menzies thinks some more.

'OK,' he says. 'It's worth a try. Thanks.'

'Follow me,' I whisper. 'And bring the letter.'

We creep out of my room, tiptoe across the landing and into Mum and Dad's room. I close the door behind us and switch the light on.

Mum and Dad are asleep, tangled up in the sheets. We're all messy sleepers in our family.

'Mum,' I say. 'Dad. There's something important I need to ask you.'

Dad groans and opens one eye.

'Sorry,' I say. 'But it's urgent. Me and Menzies won't be able to sleep till we know the answer.'

'Bridget,' moans Mum long-sufferingly. Then she sits up, alarmed. 'Is something wrong?'

'Can I have a note for school?' I say. 'So I can go to Canberra with Menzies next weekend?'

'Canberra?' says Mum, staring at us both. 'Why?'

'To meet my parents,' says Menzies. 'So they can repay your hospitality.'

I take it back, porridge doesn't make you slow after all.

Mum and Dad look at each other. I can see they're both delighted.

'Of course you can,' says Mum. 'How exciting.' Then a thought hits her. 'How will you get there?'

'Dave'll drive us,' says Menzies. 'Then he can visit his mum.'

Mum looks at Dad. He shrugs, then nods. I can see they're both having visions of me and Menzies getting married and me ending up a member of parliament.

'School might prefer you didn't have two weekends away in a row,' says Mum. 'Why not make it the weekend after?'

'We can't,' I say. 'It's urgent. We need to ask Menzies' dad to get some kids out of a refugee detention centre.'

Mum and Dad look at each other again. Suddenly they don't seem quite so delighted.

'A refugee detention centre?' says Dad.

'I don't think you should be getting mixed up in that sort of thing,' says Mum doubtfully. 'Those detention centres are there for a reason. The government's explained it all. They're to scare off other refugees who might be thinking of coming here.'

'Mum's right,' says Dad.

Sometimes Mum and Dad are so trusting and law-abiding I could scream.

'There are kids locked up in those places,' I say. 'Little kids with toothache. Older brothers who are desperate.'

I turn to Menzies for help.

'My father likes to hear citizens' views on government policy,' says Menzies. 'Plus we've got loads of spare rooms at our place, so it won't be a problem.'

Mum and Dad still look doubtful.

'Show them the letter, Menzies,' I say.

Menzies holds out the letter.

'The hunger strike bit,' I say. 'Show them the hunger strike bit.'

Menzies points to one of the pages. Dad takes it, and he and Mum read it.

'Jeez,' says Dad. 'Kids on a hunger strike.'

'Bridget, love,' says Mum, looking

pretty shocked too. 'There are some awful things happening in the world, and it's very sad, but there's not a lot we can do. We've got our own families to worry about. Isn't that right, Len?'

Dad doesn't answer for a bit. He's staring at the page. Then he realises Mum is looking at him. 'Yeah,' he says.

But he doesn't sound convinced.

'You know what'll happen if those kids don't eat,' he says to Mum. 'The authorities'll stick plastic tubes down their throats, right down into their guts, and pump food into 'em.'

Mum looks even more unhappy.

Menzies is looking aghast.

I wish he hadn't had to hear that. It's always a shock for people who don't have anything to do with jails. Particularly when they hear how the plastic tubes make the bile rush up the hunger strikers' throats and burn the inside of their noses.

But it's probably just as well Menzies has heard it because now he knows exactly what Jamal and Bibi are facing.

# CHAPTER THIRTEEN

The time is approximately 8.12 a.m. and I'm proceeding in a westerly direction across our living room towards the kitchen.

Something is wrong.

I can feel it in my guts.

I try and work out what it can be.

Menzies is having a shower upstairs, but I've removed all the illegal toiletries from the upstairs bathroom so that's OK. Dave the bodyguard is using the shower next to the laundry, but I've made sure the soap and toothpaste in there are legal and the fake serial numbers on the washing machine and dryer are facing the wall so that's OK too.

Hang on, I think I know what might be wrong.

'Mum,' I whisper urgently, leaning across the kitchen benchtop. 'Where's Dad?'

Mum stops scrambling eggs and rolls her eyes.

'The warehouse,' she says. 'He kept me awake half the night tossing and turning and then he was up at seven with some harebrained scheme about sending a gift to every member of parliament. Something about persuading them to change their minds about keeping kids in detention centres.'

'Oh no,' I say.

'You're telling me,' says Mum. 'He's left us alone in the house with a federal policeman.'

I'm thinking of something much more awful than that. I'm thinking of Uncle Grub backing his van up to the side door of parliament house. I'm thinking of government ministers going ballistic when they see Dad's gifts have got fake serial numbers and instructing Dave to arrest our whole family.

There's no time to explain this to Mum.

I grab the phone.

'It's Sunday,' says Mum. 'The warehouse answering machine'll be on.'

'I'll ring his mobile,' I say.

Mum points to Dad's mobile on the kitchen bench.

It's my turn to roll my eyes. Dad's memory is a shoddily-made imitation of the genuine article.

'We've got to go to the warehouse,' I say.

'I can't,' says Mum. 'I can't just leave our visitors here.'

She points upstairs and I know she's referring to Iraqi pressure cookers, among other things.

I feel like I'm in an Iraqi pressure cooker myself. 'I'll go,' I say. 'I know the way. I'll see you in a bit.

Before Mum can stop me I'm out the front door and hurrying down the street. I'm pretty sure I know the way. I've never done it on foot before, but I've memorised most of the landmarks in case me and Dad are ever in a police chase and he gets wounded and I have to take the wheel and drive to the warehouse to destroy all the incriminating evidence before the police get there. I've never worked out exactly how I'll do it because there's heaps of the stuff and burning it would attract too much attention and flushing it down the dunny would take months and burying it would take almost as . . .

What's that noise behind me?

It's a car, crawling along at my heel, following me.

I daren't turn round. If it's the police they'll tell from my face I'm guilty.

'Bridget. Hop in.'

It's Menzies' voice.

I turn round. Menzies is grinning at me out of the passenger window of Dave's car. Dave is at the wheel, looking like most adults do when their Sunday morning is being ruined by kids.

'We told your Mum we'd give you a lift,' says Menzies.

'Thanks,' I mumble and get in.

What is Mum thinking of? Letting a federal policeman and the son of a government minister go to the warehouse? But I guess if she'd tried to stop them that would have given the game away too.

Boy, it's complicated being a criminal.

For a second I'm tempted to give

them wrong directions and pretend I'm just going to the video shop or something, but then I remember I've got to stop Dad.

'We're going to where Dad works,' I say and start giving directions.

'Not so fast,' says Dave. 'I'm not a taxi driver.'

I'm glad he's not because the couple of times we get lost gives me extra time to think about how I can stop them actually going into the warehouse.

By the time we turn into the industrial estate, I know how.

'Sorry,' I say as we park outside the warehouse. 'Dad's very strict on security and only people with security clearance can go in. I won't be long.'

I slip out of the car and hurry into the warehouse. The others don't follow. I'm not surprised. I was pretty sure Dave would respect security arrangements.

Dad is up the back, dusting off a sewing machine with a rag.

'G'day, love,' he says with a grin. 'Did Mum tell you about my plan?'

'Yes,' I say.

'Best sewing machine made in Romania, this little beauty,' says Dad. 'Seriously top-notch.' He points to a pile of them stacked on pallets. 'I've got enough to send one to every politician in Canberra. They'll save a fortune on clothing alterations and repairs. Show them a little kindness and they might find it a bit easier to show some kindness to those locked-up kiddies, that's how I see it.'

'Dad,' I say. 'I wish you were Prime Minister.'

Dad looks pleased.

'But,' I go on, 'you can't do it. It's too risky. What if a government department decides to check where these sewing machines came from? And then everything else in here?'

I point to all the shelves of stuff.

Dad thinks about this. He waves the idea away.

'Government departments,' he says scornfully. 'They're hopeless. Take 'em years to work it out.'

'But what if they're not all hopeless?' I say. 'What if Dave's department works it out while I'm in Canberra?'

Dad thinks about that. His shoulders sag.

'Sorry, love,' he says. 'Didn't occur to me it might put you in the poo. I'll leave it till you get back. Jeez, I got a bit carried away, didn't I? I'm glad Mum sent you down here.'

I nod. Best not to say anything.

Dad's face darkens. 'But I'm gunna write to those politicians,' he says. 'Not on paper from here, from the newsagents. Tell them what I think about them locking up kids.'

I give Dad a hug. 'I'm really proud you're my dad,' I say.

He squeezes me tight. 'Good luck in Canberra,' he says.

Once again I don't say anything. This time it's because I'm distracted by what I see when I peer past Dad's armpit.

Menzies, standing in the loading bay of the warehouse, staring at me and Dad.

He sees me looking at him and turns away and pretends to be studying all the stuff on the shelves. Right near him is a pile of fake *Lord of the Rings* t-shirts and doona covers.

Now he's staring at a shipping container. Or rather one particular part of the container.

The big patch of shiny raw metal where the serial number used to be before it was illegally removed with a power grinder.

## CHAPTER FOURTEEN

'Bridget White, perhaps you can help us with our enquiries.'

The voice is so loud I nearly jump out of my chair. Mr Creely is standing by my desk, staring down at me.

Science class.

He wants an answer, but what was the question?

Desperately I try to clear my head of all the questions I've just been thinking about. Whether Menzies' parents will let us go to Canberra this weekend. Why Menzies has been avoiding me for the last two days since we got back from my place.

'I and the rest of the class are rather

hoping,' says Mr Creely, 'that you'll supply us with some information. Concerning the matter I've been talking about for the last ten minutes.'

My brain feels like the cotton wool that Bangladeshi hearing-aids come packed in.

'Or shall I just give you a weekend detention for daydreaming?' says Mr Creely.

Antoinette is signalling to me frantically. She's mouthing something.

Parachutes?

'Parasites,' I say, suddenly remembering.

'Thank you, Antoinette,' says Mr Creely. 'Now, Miss White, as I'm sure you know, parasites are organisms that take what they need for their survival from other organisms. I've just been explaining, as I'm sure you're aware, that there are many more parasite species on our planet than non-parasite species. So, to avoid a detention this weekend, please name one parasite species that nobody else has mentioned in this class today.'

I stare at him in panic.

Now my brain doesn't even feel as intelligent as cotton wool.

A flicker of something Dad once said comes back to me.

'Fungus,' I blurt out. 'There's a species of fungus that lives in mud around the Turkmenistan/Uzbekistan border and gets under your toenails and makes them drop off which is a real problem for the truckdrivers because they can't push their trucks out of mudslides and the bandits will only tow you out if you give them half your load except they're not interested in DVD players that aren't multi-zone . . .'

My brain catches up with my gabbling mouth and I stop.

I've already said way too much.

Mr Creely is looking a bit stunned.

The rest of the class are staring.

The bell goes. Mr Creely shakes his head, turns away and dismisses us.

I wait till everyone's gone, praying that none of the other kids understood what I was really saying. Then I step out into the corridor.

Menzies is waiting for me.

Behind his glasses his eyes are big and troubled. My insides go into more knots than a Romanian hammock.

'My mother called back,' he says. 'We can go to Canberra this weekend.'

'That's great,' I say, but I can see there's more to come.

'First,' says Menzies, 'there's some stuff I need to know. What exactly does your father do in his business?'

'Not here,' I say, glancing anxiously up and down the corridor. 'Let's talk in your room.'

We go to his room. On the way I silently rehearse all my emergency excuses about Dad. How he's not good at paperwork, specially import dockets. How he's always losing receipts. How the serial number of the container got accidently scraped off when he bumped it with an Uzbekistan cheese grater.

None of it sounds very true.

We go into Menzies' room and Menzies closes the door.

'Bridget,' he says, looking unhappy. 'Is your father a criminal?'

I feel extremely unhappy he's asked, but I try not to show it, even though my

99

chest is thudding harder than a Bosnian lawnmower.

'A criminal?' I say. 'What makes you think that?'

'The stuff you came out with in class,' says Menzies. 'DVD players on the Afghanistan border or whatever it was.'

'That's just stuff I know about,' I say. 'It doesn't make my dad a criminal.'

'And the *Lord of the Rings* doona covers in your father's warehouse,' says Menzies. 'I know they aren't genuine because in the movie Frodo isn't Asian.'

We look at each other and I don't know what to say.

It's a fair cop.

My legs feel like they're turning into Bulgarian jelly, the stuff you have to drink through a straw.

This is what I've dreaded for years. This is why I've never made a real friend. This is why I shouldn't have made this one.

Part of me wishes I'd never met Menzies. But something confusing is happening. Another part of me wants to tell him the truth.

'Hang on,' I say. 'I'll be back.'

I go out into the corridor and knock on Dave the bodyguard's door. It opens. Dave looks down at me, his eyebrows asking me what I want.

'Dave,' I say. 'You know that blender my uncle gave you? Me and Menzies were wondering if you could make us a smoothie.'

Dave thinks about this.

'And what'll happen if I don't?' he says. 'Will your dad shoot me?'

For a second I think he's serious, but then he grins. 'Only joking,' he says. 'Banana or Milo?'

'Both,' I say. 'Thanks.'

I go back into Menzies' room and shut the door. Menzies starts to speak, but I put my finger to my lips. We wait in silence till the roar of the Russian blender starts up next door.

Perfect. Nobody could hear us now even if they were trying to.

I'm still not sure what's going to happen next. Menzies interrogating me, or me confessing to him.

Then suddenly there's something I

want more than anything else in the world.

One friend I can be honest with.

I turn to Menzies.

'Do you promise not to blab to your dad or anyone else in the government what I'm about to tell you?' I say.

Menzies hesitates. Only for a second.

'I promise,' he says.

I dig my fingernails into my palms. It's an old burglar trick to give you courage.

'My dad is a sort of criminal,' I say. 'He doesn't steal and he doesn't do violence, but most of the stuff in his warehouse did fall off the back of trucks overseas.'

'I thought so,' says Menzies quietly.

I keep going.

'Our family doesn't do armed robbery,' I say firmly. 'Or breaking and entering. Except Uncle Grub when he was first married but he regrets it now. And we don't steal cars or sell drugs or kidnap people.'

I stop. Confessions are really hard. Harder than secrets sometimes.

Menzies just looks at me.

'If you don't want to be friends with a crim kid,' I say, 'or take one to your place, I'll understand.'

Menzies frowns. I can see he's having deep thoughts. Maybe one day he'll be Prime Minister.

After what seems like several years, he finally speaks.

'I do want to be your friend,' he says.

I struggle not to look too relieved.

'But,' Menzies goes on, 'there is a problem.'

Just as well I kept the relief under control.

'Dave is a federal police officer,' says Menzies. 'He's trained to spot crime. Isn't it too risky, you being around him?'

The noise of the Russian blender fades away and so do the knots inside me. So that's all Menzies is worried about.

'I'm used to risks,' I say.

Telling Menzies about my family was the big risk. Dave I can cope with.

'It'll be fine,' I say. 'If he was going to arrest my family he'd have done it last weekend at the party.'

Menzies gives me a relieved smile.

I grin back.

Good old Dad. It's what he's always told me. Honesty is the best policy.

## CHAPTER FIFTEEN

People are kind.

I've always believed that, even when sometimes they do things that aren't kind. For example Uncle Ray was burgled once and as well as taking his TV and video, the burglar did a poo on his couch.

That wasn't very kind.

I reckon the burglar was just jealous. He'd heard about all the doctor and vet work Uncle Ray does and the burglar was jealous that he'd never had the chance to go to university and make something of himself. Poor bloke, he didn't need to be jealous. Uncle Ray didn't go to university either.

Dave the bodyguard is very kind.

He's just spent hours and hours driving us to Canberra. OK, it's his job but he still didn't have to. He could have taken a sickie or pretended it was too much of a security risk because of terrorists posing as petrol station employees.

Menzies is kind too.

When me and Dave said we were sick of playing *I Spy*, Menzies didn't whinge or get cross, he just said if I was feeling tired I could sleep on his shoulder. That was very kind, even though he immediately fell asleep on mine.

And now we're in Canberra, driving along the dark streets towards Menzies' place, I can see that the people here are kind too.

The big buildings are all lit up at night so visitors don't bang into them in the dark.

The lawns around the buildings are all neatly clipped so small children don't wander off and get lost in the undergrowth.

And all over the lawns, nibbling the grass and cooling down in the sprinklers, are hundreds and hundreds of kangaroos.

Only very kind people would share their city with hungry creatures that have come in from the bush. People with good and caring hearts. Which is why I'm sure that when we get to Menzies' place and I ask his dad to help Jamal and Bibi, his dad'll say yes.

## CHAPTER SIXTEEN

'So, Bridget,' says Menzies' dad, smiling at me across the dining table. 'What are you and Menzies planning to do in Canberra?'

I don't answer straight away because I've got a mouthful of genuine lobster and I don't want to risk spraying any on a government minister. Or on the walls of a genuine luxury apartment. Or on any of the other guests who all look like international supermodels and managing directors and ambassadors from exotic countries.

While I chew I look pleadingly at Menzies, hoping he'll answer.

I can't see him too clearly because

there's a big cluster of candles in the middle of the table. Through the wobbling flames he looks like he's feeling a bit overwhelmed by everything too. His parents, their friends, the size of the dining table, everything.

I don't blame him.

The knives and forks here are genuine stainless steel, all the way through. The serviettes are genuine cloth with real embroidery, not just printed on. The plates are bone china, I checked underneath. The really good quality bone china, not the stuff from Bulgaria. These are probably from China.

Everyone around the table is looking at me.

'Do you want to visit the National Gallery?' says Menzies' dad. 'The Science Museum? The Institute of Sport?'

I swallow the lobster.

'Actually,' I say, 'we want to ask you a favour.'

Menzies' dad glances at Menzies' mum, who gives a little shrug.

'Everyone wants a favour from the minister,' says one of the guests.

The others all laugh.

'Be fair,' Menzies' dad says to them. 'She's got just as much right as anyone. She'll be voting in a few years.'

The others all chuckle.

I feel my face getting hot. Through the candlelight, I see Menzies is feeling the same. His face looks the same colour as the lobster shell on his plate.

'Ask away, my dear,' says Menzies' dad to me. 'In this country every voter has a right to be heard. I'm only a humble minister of the crown, but I'll do everything in my power to grant your request.'

Some of the supermodels and ambassadors applaud.

"The children in the detention centres,' I say. 'We'd like you to set them free, please.'

The room goes very quiet, except for Menzies' mum who puts her knife and fork onto her plate with a tiny noise.

Menzies' dad gives a sigh.

'I wish I could, Bridget,' he says. 'But I'm just one member of a team. A team called the government. And it was a decision by the whole team that people who try to get into Australia without permission must be locked up.'

I glance across at Menzies. He's staring at his dad and in the flickering candlelight he looks like he's almost in tears.

I open my mouth to tell Menzies' dad about Bibi's toothache and Jamal's hunger strike plans and how they only came to Australia because their house was blown up and the government in Afghanistan tried to kill their parents.

Before I can, Menzies stands up and yells at his father.

'You can help them if you want to,' he shouts accusingly. 'You're a minister. You're important. But you just don't want to. You don't care. All you care about is staying elected.'

He stops, panting for breath.

The adults around the table are staring at him, horrified.

All except Menzies' father. His face, as he stares at Menzies, is sad.

Menzies' mum stands up and steers me gently out of my chair.

'Come on, children,' she says quietly. 'Time for bed. The minister's got a very busy night. He's going back to the house soon for an all-night sitting. I think we should give him some time to say goodbye to his guests.'

As she guides me and Menzies to the door, the guests at the table all start talking at once.

'What about that girl?' says a woman's voice. 'How rude to come here and attack you like that. I blame the parents. It's criminal.'

Menzies' father's voice is softer, and weary. 'We've brought our son up to think for himself,' he says. 'As you can see, it's working.'

## CHAPTER SEVENTEEN

I tap on Menzies' bedroom door and creep in.

His room feels about six times bigger than his one at school. At first, in the gloom, I can't see the bed. The muffled sounds tell me where it is. As my eyes get used to the darkness, I see Menzies lying with his head under his pillow.

I've been pretending we're in prison and I've been giving him his space. Gavin reckons when the other bloke in the cell has a cry, it's really important to give him his space.

I don't know how Gavin does it. Menzies' muffled noises coming through the wall were so unhappy I could hardly bear it. I tried to think of other things to take my mind off it, but all I could think of was Jamal lying awake at night listening to Bibi cry from toothache.

Now I'm in Menzies' room, though, I realise it's not sobbing he's doing under his pillow, it's something else.

Angry frustrated swearing.

I sit on Menzies' bed, switch on his lamp and shake his shoulder.

'Menzies,' I say. 'Put your glasses on. I've got something important to ask you.'

Menzies pulls the pillow off his head and rolls over and looks up at me.

'Politics has turned my father into a monster,' he says. 'He used to be a

111

hero. He used to help people. Pensioners and war veterans and people who didn't have enough parking spaces in their office blocks. He used to care.'

'Menzies, I say, 'when your mum said your dad was going back to the house tonight, did she mean your other house?'

'No,' mutters Menzies. 'Our other house is hundreds of kilometres away. She meant parliament house.'

'So everyone's still at parliament house,' I say. 'Working all night.'

Menzies nods.

'Good,' I say.

'No it's not,' he says. 'I don't want my father to be in politics any more. Next time there's an election, I want him to lose.'

Suddenly Menzies sits up and grabs my shoulders. Little reflections of the bedside lamp make his eyes even brighter than usual.

'Your family can help,' he says. 'Your family can send thugs to every voting booth to threaten to bash people if they vote for my father. Your family can kidnap my father's campaign manager. And burn down the place that prints his how-to-vote cards. And then . . .'

'Menzies,' I say sharply. 'My family don't do that sort of crime.'

Menzies sinks back onto his pillow.

'But,' I say, 'we can still help Jamal and Bibi.'

'How?' says Menzies gloomily.

'By asking the right person,' I say.

Menzies looks at me. I can see he doesn't get it.

'Just now we asked the wrong person,' I say.

'I know,' says Menzies, even more gloomily.

'Your dad reckons he's just a member of a team,' I say. 'The government team.'

Menzies looks at me again. He still doesn't get it. Anger does that to your brain. Turns it into Turkmenistan border mud.

'Who's the boss of the government?' I ask. Menzies' eyes widen. Now he gets it.

'The Prime Minister,' he says.

113

'Exactly,' I say. 'That's who we have to go and see.'


## CHAPTER EIGHTEEN

So far so good.

Creeping out of Menzies' place was pretty easy. The guests had all gone and his mother was asleep and Dave didn't leap out of a cupboard and arrest us. Menzies reminded me that when Dave's in Canberra he goes and stays with his mum in Belconnen and she makes him go to bed early.

Finding parliament house was pretty easy too. It's only about three streets away from Menzies' place, and it's got a huge hill on top of it so it's pretty easy to spot, even in the dark.

Getting to it isn't quite so easy. There are big roads running around the place in circles. Plus there are still quite a few cars even though it's after midnight. Canberra must have lots of nightclubs.

'Watch out,' I yell at Menzies.

I grab him and pull him out of the way of a speeding ute.

'Thanks,' he pants 'My glasses have fogged up.'

I wait for him to wipe them on his shirt, then we run across the last road and onto the big lawn sloping up to the parliament house entrance.

Suddenly I'm feeling a bit nervous.

On this huge lawn I can't see a single kangaroo. Perhaps the people in parliament house aren't as kind as the other people in Canberra.

'Menzies,' I say. 'Does the Prime Minister have bodyguards? Ones that shoot on sight if he's approached by a kangaroo or people without an appointment?'

'Don't think so,' says Menzies. 'He has bodyguards, but only when he's out in public or having the US president round for a barbie. Come on, we can get in this way.'

Menzies heads down a slope at the side of the building and I follow.

I realise what he's doing. We're going to break in round the back where we won't be noticed.

115

Suddenly I'm feeling very nervous. The night air is warm, but there's a cold dampness coming up off the grass and it's making me shiver.

When I was little, Dad used to tell me a story about a gang of evil robbers who had a huge fortress under a hill where they kept all their gold and jewels and frequent flyer points. It was so heavily guarded it was impossible to break into unless you had a magic horse with wings and a diesel excavator.

The closer we get, the more parliament house is reminding me of that place. Trouble is, me and Menzies don't have any heavy earth-moving equipment. And I've left the master key Uncle Ollie gave me in my locker at school.

I take some deep breaths to steady my nerves.

I think of Jamal and Bibi, trapped in a different sort of evil fortress, desperate for our help.

My heart starts to beat faster. Not just with fear.

With determination as well.

116

Don't be scared, I tell myself. If it was easy to drop in for a chat with the Prime Minister, everyone would be doing it.

'This way,' says Menzies.

His voice doesn't sound scared, and it makes me feel brave too.

We hurry along a concrete tunnel.

Suddenly I'm ready to do anything. Climb high walls. Crawl through sewers. Duck under security beams and hide in prickly foliage. Anything that doesn't involve snakes.

Or security guards.

I grab Menzies. At the end of the tunnel is a security checkpoint. Two guards are watching us approach.

'It's OK,' says Menzies.

He just keeps walking towards them. I follow because there's nothing else to do. I can't run and leave him to face them alone.

I'm just starting to wonder if me being shot in an underground entrance to parliament house will cause Mum and Dad to be investigated, when one of the guards speaks.

'G'day, Menzies,' he says. 'Your dad

working tonight?'

Menzies nods.

My mouth falls open. I close it in case leaving it hanging open makes me look guilty.

'You're having a late one too, eh Menzies?' says the guard. 'Best not run around outside when your dad brings you here. Some of my colleagues might not recognise you. And they might think your friend's a terrorist.'

The other security guard gives me a grin.

My legs are trembling harder than an Armenian sandwich-toaster struggling bravely to toast a sandwich.

The first security guard signals for us to step through the metal detector.

I have a horrible thought.

What if I've got any illegal items on me? Mum and Dad could end up the victims of a major crime investigation even without me being shot.

I pat my pockets, thinking fast. My Bulgarian gameboy is back at school. My Latvian walkman is with one of my cousins after her Japanese one broke. I'm not wearing a fake *Lord of the*

*Rings* t-shirt.

Phew, all clear.

I step through the metal detector. Menzies does too.

The alarm doesn't go off.

'House will be sitting for hours yet,' says the first guard. 'Pop into the visitors' gallery and give your dad a wave.'

'Thanks, Dennis,' says Menzies.

Weak with relief, I give Dennis and the other guard my friendliest smile and check that I haven't wet myself.

Then me and Menzies walk into parliament house.


## CHAPTER NINETEEN

The time is approximately 12.23 a.m. and we're proceeding along a corridor in the actual genuine parliament house of Australia.

I'm not sure what direction we're going. Towards the Prime Minister I hope.

'Do you know where to find him?' I

ask.

'I think so,' says Menzies. 'Dad used to bring me here when I was little. Before he got too busy. I think the Prime Minister's office is round this corner.'

I stop at the corner and peek into the next corridor.

All clear.

Except for the security cameras everywhere. The people who run our school should see this. Give them some clues about protecting their vases.

I have a scary thought.

What if we're being video taped? What if there's a government department that checks the family background of every visitor to parliament house for security reasons?

As I follow Menzies down the corridor I make my cheeks bulge out so the government won't recognise me if they've got copies of my old school photos. Uncle Grub does the same thing when he drives past speed cameras.

'Here it is,' says Menzies. 'The Prime Minister's office.' He squints at me.

'Are you OK?'

I nod and let my cheeks go back to normal.

The security guard sitting behind a desk outside the Prime Minister's office is giving me a strange look too.

Menzies pulls a plastic ID card from his pocket and shows it to the guard.

'We'd like a quick word with the Prime Minister, please,' he says.

This security guard doesn't look as friendly as Dennis. He shakes his head.

'I'm not at liberty to divulge the PM's whereabouts,' he says.

Menzies' face falls. He whispers in my ear. 'He's saying he can't tell us where the Prime Minister is.'

I look at the office door behind the guard. It's shut and no light is coming through the crack at the bottom. Either the Prime Minister is in there playing his gameboy in the dark or he's somewhere else.

'Does the Prime Minister have a gameboy?' I ask the guard.

The guard looks at me steadily.

'I'm not at liberty to divulge any information about the PM,' he says.

Is that a hint of a smile on his face? Or indigestion?

'Thanks, anyway,' I say.

I turn to Menzies.

'I don't think the Prime Minister's in there,' I say. As we head back the way we came I try to think what to do next.

'Have you got the Prime Minister's number?' I say to Menzies. 'We could ring him on your mobile.'

Menzies shakes his head. 'He's unlisted. But he's the boss of this place, so he must be around here somewhere.'

In the distance I can hear the humming of machinery. I hope it's not a senator using a Turkish electric shaver Dad sent here without telling me.

We hurry down the corridor and round another corner.

I see what's making the noise. A man in overalls operating a floor polisher.

'Excuse me,' says Menzies to the cleaner. 'Do you know where the Prime Minister is?'

The cleaner doesn't say anything or switch his machine off. He just points to a big door further down the corridor.

'Thanks,' says Menzies.

He sprints towards the door. I follow. For a second I'm not sure why we're running. Then I realise. This is all taking too long. If Menzies' mum wakes up and finds us gone, she'll ring Dave and we could be sprung at any moment.

Menzies reaches the door and raises his hand to knock.

'No time for that,' I say.

I give the door a big heave and we both go in.

My first thought is that we've walked into a courtroom. There's an important-looking bloke sitting up one end just like when Gavin was in court. And a long table with people standing at it.

But this place is much bigger than Gavin's courtroom. And all the seats are green. There are loads of them sloping up on both sides. And there are loads of people sitting in them.

'Oh, poop,' breathes Menzies next to me. I know what he means.

I've seen this on TV.

This is the actual genuine parliament of Australia.

My guts turn to Albanian powdered mashed potato. I want to run. But I don't. I think of Jamal and Bibi.

There's a big Australian coat of arms on the wall just like in Gavin's courtroom. This isn't a court but it looks like a place of justice and that's what Jamal and Bibi need.

I go over to the table and peer up at all the faces. They're all looking at me now. One of them must be the Prime Minister but my blood's beating so hard in my eyeballs I can't recognise him.

If I speak to them all he'll be included.

'Your honours and worships,' I say as loud as I can.

I don't know if that's right but I hope it is.

'Jamal and Bibi didn't do anything wrong. It's not fair to lock them up. They're not criminals, they're just kids.'

All the members of parliament are

staring at me. They look shocked. Perhaps they thought Jamal and Bibi were drunk drivers or something.

The bloke up the end stands up. I can see he's not the Prime Minister, but he looks like he fancies himself.

'Security,' he yells. 'Remove these children from the house.'

Oh, no. They're going to chuck us out. They don't care about Jamal and Bibi.

'Wait,' roars a voice next to me. 'Listen.'

It's Menzies. I can't believe it. I've never heard him yell so loud.

'I know you're not really cruel and mean,' says Menzies, blinking up at the rows of politicians. 'You're just scared cause there's so many millions of refugees in the world. You're scared that if you're kind to the few that are here, all the others will want to come. Well it's OK, they can come.'

The members of parliament are all staring at Menzies now, a bit stunned.

'Look at America,' continues Menzies. 'They've got nearly three hundred million people. Australia's almost as big as America and we've only got twenty million people. So we've got heaps of room for refugees. They'll build new cities for us. New industries. Make us successful at soccer. My dad will arrange it. He's Minister for National Development.'

Menzies stops, out of breath.

I want to hug him.

'Here, here,' I yell.

But none of the members of parliament yell it. They've all stopped staring at Menzies and now they're looking at someone sitting in a front seat near the table.

Menzies' father.

Everyone starts laughing. The whole place rocks with roars and howls of laughter.

Then I see some people aren't laughing.

The official bloke up the end of the table isn't. Nor is Menzies' father. He's glaring at Menzies in a fury.

Menzies isn't laughing either. He looks like he's only just realising what he's done.

The other people not laughing are

the two security guards, neither of them Dennis, who are lunging towards us.

## CHAPTER TWENTY

I grab Menzies and drag him towards the door.

Members of parliament jump to their feet to get a better look at us. Some of them, because they're very important and like to be at the front, get in the way of the security guards.

I heave the door open, haul Menzies out and look frantically for an escape route.

There isn't one.

The corridor is full of people running towards us from both directions.

Not security guards.

Journalists.

They surround us, yelling questions and taking pictures.

'What's your name?'

'How old are you?'

'Who made you do this?'

The journalists are packed in so tight the security guards can't reach us. But I don't feel relieved because I've just seen something even scarier than security guards.

On my wrist.

My watch.

It's a Cartier ladies watch. Cartier is a top-notch company in France and their watches cost thousands. Trouble is, mine was made in Taiwan. I forgot about it when we went through the metal detector. Luckily it didn't set the alarm off, probably because it hasn't got much real metal in it. Dad's got heaps of them in his warehouse. If anyone from Cartier finds out, Dad's in big trouble.

I've got to throw these journalists off the scent. I start by putting my hand behind my back. 'Come on, sweetie,' yells a reporter waving a voice recorder. 'What's your name?'

I assume he's talking to me because Menzies just told the whole of parliament who his family is.

'Britney Spears,' I say. It's the first

name that comes into my head. I hope she doesn't mind.

'Where do you live,' shouts another reporter.

'Turkmenistan,' I say.

If Dad finds out I've been telling all these lies he'll be really upset, even though I'm only doing it to keep him out of jail. That's the trouble with having such an honest dad.

'What are you trying to achieve?' says a lady journalist who looks as if she's already decided we're totally mad and has already written that in her notebook.

'We're trying to see the Prime Minister,' I say. 'We're trying to ask him to stop locking kids up.'

'Well, young lady,' says an angry voice. 'You're going to get your wish because the Prime Minister wants to see you right now.'

It's Menzies' father, forcing himself through the circle of journalists.

He grabs me and Menzies.

'Give them a break,' he snaps at the journalists. 'They're just kids.'

From the grim look on his face, I can

see he still feels pretty upset about everyone laughing at him. As he drags us both down the corridor, I hope the Prime Minister's in a better mood.

## CHAPTER TWENTY-ONE

The Prime Minister is in a much better mood.

He invites me and Menzies to sit down in his office and gives us a drink from his fridge, which is pretty good of him because as a rule he probably has servants to do that sort of thing.

So far he hasn't stopped smiling.

'I know you of course, Menzies,' he says. He turns to me. 'And you're . . . ?'

'Bridget,' I say.

No point in lying. The Prime Minister probably knows Britney Spears personally.

'Bridget White,' says Menzies' father, who's standing next to us looking pretty sour. After what he's just been through in parliament, I think he deserves a drink too.

'Well, Bridget and Menzies,' says the Prime Minister. 'You've had quite a night.'

Menzies, who's looking a bit pale and ill, doesn't say anything. Neither do I. For now I'm concentrating on trying to sit naturally with my watch wrist behind my back.

'I want to thank you both,' says the Prime Minister. 'For alerting me to a couple of weaknesses in our security. As a result of your escapade tonight, two members of the parliamentary security service will be suspended and retrained. Also, until further notice, I am forbidding members of parliament or parliamentary staff to have any family visitors here. Which means this year's Christmas party for the children of parliamentarians will be cancelled.'

Even though the things he's saying are angry things, he's still smiling.

That is so dishonest.

'I hope you're both satisfied,' says Menzies' father.

At least he looks angry. I know he's a big disappointment to Menzies, but at least Menzies can see he's not as dishonest as the Prime Minister.

'That's all,' says the Prime Minister. 'Unless you have anything you want to say.'

'Yes, I do,' I reply. 'I want to know why you lock innocent children up.'

As soon as the words come out I know I've let Jamal and Bibi down.

This is the Prime Minister. He's used to people saying please. He's used to people saying if you could possibly be so generous as to consider our request your honour we'd be extremely incredibly grateful.

Why couldn't I have said that?

I should be arrested sometimes.

Oh well, at least he's looking angry now, so what he's about to say will probably be the truth.

'Mandatory detention,' says the Prime Minister, 'is a crucial element in a sophisticated immigration strategy whose positive outcomes are not always apparent to the unsophisticated.'

I try to work out what that means.

I can't.

The Prime Minister takes our drinks

from us and puts them on his desk, signals for us to stand and ushers us towards the door.

Menzies' father takes a step forward.

'They are both very sorry for the embarrassment they've caused,' he says, looking at me and Menzies. 'Aren't you?'

I don't say anything. Neither does Menzies. The Prime Minister opens the door.

'No need to apologise,' he says. 'I'm not embarrassed. When opponents of my government's policies increase their worldly experience and cognitive ability, they understand that border protection is an initiative wholly in the national interest.'

He shuts the door behind us.

Once again I try to work out what he meant. I haven't got a clue.

'Menzies,' I whisper as we follow his father past the expressionless security guard and into the corridor. 'What did that stuff about positive outcomes and unsophisticated mean?'

'The Prime Minster was saying,' replies Menzies, 'that the government is big and knows what's best, and we're little and we don't.'

Now I understand.

I think the Prime Minster's wrong. And rude.

He should meet Gavin, who could tell him how dopey it is to plead not guilty when you are.

'And,' I say to Menzies, 'what did the Prime Minister mean when he said all that stuff about national interest?'

'He meant that the government's doing it for us,' says Menzies.

I stare at him.

Menzies can see I still don't understand. He's frowning, like he's trying to come up with a clearer way of putting it.

'The Prime Minister reckons they're locking those kids up for us,' says Menzies. 'The people of Australia.'

'Us?' I say. 'You and me?'

'Yes,' says Menzies.

I'm so stunned I don't notice at first what Menzies' father is doing. Steering us into an office. His office, judging by the photo of Menzies' mum and Menzies on the desk.

We all sit down on a couple of couches. Menzies' father looks hard at Menzies.

'What you did tonight was wrong,' says Menzies' father. 'Very wrong.'

He seems to be talking only to Menzies, who's staring at the carpet.

'When I was your age,' continues Menzies' father, 'I wouldn't have dreamed of doing something like that. Something that would cause my father shame and embarrassment. No matter how passionately I felt about an issue.'

He stops, and now he's staring at the carpet too. Menzies looks so miserable I want to put my arm round him.

'That's why,' says Menzies' father, 'as well as feeling angry, I feel a tiny bit jealous.'

There's a silence.

I try and work out if I heard that right.

Menzies has obviously decided he did.

He's staring at his father in shock.

His father reaches over and squeezes Menzies' shoulder.

This is fantastic. Perhaps Menzies'

father is going to help Jamal and Bibi after all. I can see Menzies is hoping the same thing.

'I wanted you to know that,' says Menzies' father. 'There are two other things I want you to know. One, I can't change the government's policy on refugees, not now, not ever.'

Menzies sags in his seat.

I do too.

'Two,' says Menzies' father, and suddenly he's looking at me with a stern expression.

'In this life,' he says, 'be very careful who you choose as friends.'


## CHAPTER TWENTY-TWO

On the long drive back to school, Menzies doesn't feel like talking.

Neither does Dave. He looks at me a few times in the rear-vision mirror. Maybe he's going to be suspended too.

I wonder if I should offer to write him a reference.

*To Whom It May Concern. Dave is a*

*very good bodyguard and a pleasure to be guarded by. The only reason he didn't stop us getting into parliament house is he was visiting his mum.*

Something like that.

I decide not to. Dave is driving very fast and I don't want to risk making him swerve.

After a while, Menzies gives me something. It's a letter from Jamal.

'It came yesterday,' he says. 'We were both trying to get our homework done so Mr Galbraith would give us a weekend pass and I forgot to show you.'

'That's OK,' I say. 'I understand.'

We both had a lot of homework, thanks to Mr Creely. And sometimes Menzies prefers to have his feelings about Jamal and Bibi in private.

I read the letter.

*Dear Menzies,*

*I have bad news. My father is free. Two days ago the government gave him a visa. They have decided he is a real refugee, but they say Bibi and me and Mum are not real refugees and we have to stay in this detention centre.*

*Dad did not want to go, but they made him. He told us he is going to Adelaide to try and find a lawyer to help us. That is good, I guess, but he was very sad.*

*We are sad too, and scared. Almost like when me and Bibi got separated from Mum and Dad on the boat journey and we thought a pirate was going to kill us because Bibi called him a camel wart.*

*Bibi still gets tooth-ache most days. I am still trying to arrange the soccer match. It is going quite well. Three guards have said they will play, and twenty-seven refugees. Bibi and I may have to play on the guard team. Bibi says she would rather have all her teeth kicked out by a camel.*

*Thank you for the wonderful soccer ball, Menzies. It arrived yesterday. The guards cut it open to look for bombs, so I will repair it for our match. Don't worry, we can still train with a plastic bag ball. Sometimes I can do twenty foot-knee-heads before my hip hurts too much.*

*I try to stay hopeful, but this prison is an agony place. The man who tried to escape last month stood at the fence for six hours today, shouting at the government office over and over.*

*'When you hurt a child once,'* he shouted, *'you feel bad. When you hurt a child twice, you feel not so bad. When you hurt a child three times, you feel nothing.'*

*It's the same in soccer. Some players are sad if they hurt another player's ankle or heart. But some don't care. They feel nothing.*

*At home I saw people who hurt children and they weren't sad. They put their arms in the air like a winning team.*

*I think there are people like this in Australia too. I am sad because I thought Australia was a kind place. You are kind, Menzies.*

*You give me wings.*

*I wish they were real.*

*Your friend,*

*Jamal*

I finish reading the letter for the third time as the car jolts to a stop. We're at a petrol station.

'Toilet?' says Dave.

Menzies shakes his head.

So do I.

Dave gets out of the car.

139

'We can still help Jamal and Bibi,' I say to Menzies.

For a second Menzies' eyes flicker with hope. 'How?' he says.

Then his shoulders slump.

'It's hopeless,' he says. 'You saw how my father is. He's not brave enough to help Jamal and Bibi. The Prime Minister doesn't even care about them. And the whole Australian parliament thinks it's just a big joke.'

'You're right,' I say, glancing over to make sure Dave is still in the Men's and can't hear what I'm about to say. 'The Prime Minister doesn't care. But thanks to him I've realised what we have to do.'

'Write to the Pope?' says Menzies gloomily.

I shake my head again.

'The Prime Minister reckons they're doing all this for us,' I say. 'Well, if Jamal and Bibi are being kept prisoner for us, I reckon we've got a responsibility to do something about it ourselves.'

Menzies stares at me, his eyes almost bigger than his glasses.

140

'You mean . . . ?'

'Yes,' I say. 'We'll organise a jail break.'


## CHAPTER TWENTY-THREE

'I've found it,' I say.

I heave the big school library atlas over to where Menzies is sitting at a school library computer.

'You've found the detention centre?' says Menzies.

'Not exactly,' I say. 'They don't print detention centres in school atlases. But look, this is the highway junction near it.'

I point to the atlas and then to the computer screen. The same highway junction is on the map of the detention centre on the Department of Immigration website.

'Which means,' I say, pointing to the middle of the atlas page, 'the detention centre is here.'

It's right out in the desert,' says Menzies, dismayed. 'How are we going to get there?'

That's exactly what I'm thinking.

'I can't even go to the toilet without Dave knowing,' says Menzies.

'One problem at a time,' I say. 'At least we know where the detention centre is.'

Always locate your target first, that's what Uncle Grub used to say in his burgling days. Though he used to stick to targets near bus stops.

'Look at the fence,' says Menzies, clicking on the website and bringing up a photo of the detention centre. 'It's about five metres high, with razor-wire on top.'

'We'll have to tunnel our way in,' I say.

We both stare at the screen in silence.

I wonder if I should mention to Menzies that I'm hopeless at tunnels. At the beach, when I try to do an underground carpark, my sandcastle always collapses even when Dad tries to prop it up with a Bulgarian boogie board.

I glance at Menzies. From his

worried expression, I'd say he's accidently buried a few crabs himself. Then I have an idea.

'Jamal and Bibi's dad,' I say. 'He could help us.'

'Yes,' says Menzies, eyes lighting up. 'He's probably had experience tunnelling in the desert in Afghanistan. You know, for water or to get out of his house after a sandstorm.'

For a few seconds we're both very excited. Then I remember something.

'We only know he's somewhere in Adelaide,' I say. 'How can we find him?'

'Easy,' says Menzies. 'I'll write to Jamal and get his phone number.'

I think about this.

'It'll take too long,' I say. 'And what if the detention centre guards read Jamal's reply before they post it? They might be suspicious about why we want to contact his dad.'

'OK,' says Menzies. 'I know a kid whose mum works for the Department of Immigration. We used to go to the parliament house Christmas parties together. They've got a computer at their place connected to the department's database. The department'll definitely have a contact number for someone who's only out on a temporary visa.'

Menzies seems pretty confident, so I let myself feel confident too.

'Good one,' I say.

'I've got his number in my room,' says Menzies. 'I'll go and ring him now, before the bell goes.'

He hurries out of the library, almost knocking over a year three girl coming in with an armful of newspapers.

Jamal's right, I think to myself. You should never give up even if things are looking hopeless, and not just in soccer. Two minutes ago rescuing Jamal and Bibi seemed hopeless. Now I reckon we can do it.

The newspaper monitor girl is staring at me. Must be because it's Sunday and the librarian's not here and the kid doesn't know where to leave the papers.

I go over to give her a hand.

She's still staring at me.

'You're in the paper,' she says, and

144

runs out of the library.

I watch her go, wondering what she means. I pick up a newspaper. And almost faint.

On the front page is a huge picture of me in parliament house.

The headline is even bigger.

*CRIME GIRL BREAKS INTO POLITICS.*


## CHAPTER TWENTY-FOUR

'Look at this,' gasps Chantelle, rustling the newspaper so hard her bedsprings start to squeak. *'Bridget Podger, alias Bridget White, is the daughter of convicted criminal Leonard Reginald Podger, alias Len White, and the sister of Gavin Kenneth Podger, alias Gavin White, currently serving a jail sentence for theft.'*

I've got my head under my pillow but I can still hear her.

I wish she'd stop reading.

I wish Antoinette would too.

'Oh, no,' squeals Antoinette, rustling

her newspaper just as hard. 'Listen to this. *Bridget Podger recently enrolled at one of Australia's top private schools. Security staff say she gained entry to parliament house by posing as the friend of another student, the son of a government minister.* That's terrible.'

I bury my head deeper under my pillow and wish I hadn't brought the library newspapers up here. I should have flushed them down the dunny where they belong.

Where my life belongs, now that the one thing I've dreaded all these years has finally happened.

Menzies doesn't realise how lucky he is, having a dad who can keep him out of the papers.

'Bridget, Bridget.'

It's Veuve's frantic voice coming from the doorway. I sit up, just in case there's even worse news. When the whole country knows you're a crim, there's no limit to how bad things can get.

'Bridget,' says Veuve, coming over to help me up. 'You're on TV. Come and see.'

I give her a long hard look and she gets the message that I don't want to come and see.

Behind her the corridor is packed with kids clamouring for a glimpse of me. I poke my tongue out at them. They squeal with excitement. Chantelle closes the door in their faces.

'Donkey-brains,' she mutters.

Antoinette sits next to me on my bed and puts her arm round me. Chantelle joins her and takes my hand. Veuve comes over and squeezes my shoulder.

'You poor thing,' says Antoinette.

I stare at them, stunned. I'm a crim. From a crim family. Why are they being so nice?

'Those newspapers are a disgrace,' says Chantelle. 'Printing personal details about a person's life. They did that to my nana when she went on holiday to Surfers with an archbishop.'

'If you want to sue them,' says Veuve, 'we'll give evidence about what a good person you are and how you've never robbed us or kidnapped us.'

'Here in the stables,' says Antoinette, 'we stick together.'

I blink away tears.

For the first time I understand what it must be like for Jamal when he gets a letter from Menzies. Knowing that even when the whole world thinks you're bad, someone believes in you.

'It's not your fault what your father does,' says Chantelle. 'My father's law firm helps property developers knock old peoples' houses down. If anyone accused me of doing that, I'd spit at them.'

'My mother pollutes rivers,' says Antoinette. 'Not personally, her factories.'

'I think it sucks,' says Veuve. 'On TV they called you a mini-menace to society following in your father's footsteps.' She looks embarrassed. 'My mother's a TV journalist.'

'We think you're really brave,' says Antoinette. 'Sticking up for those kids in detention. I saw some on TV once and they were sooo cute . . .'

'Sooo cute,' say Chantelle and Veuve.

I take a deep breath to thank them all for their support, but before I can, the door bangs open and Menzies crashes into the room, eyes big and excited behind his crooked glasses.

'Bridget,' he says. 'I got through to Jamal's dad. He's going to help us.'

I don't know what to say.

The girls are all staring at Menzies.

I can see he's thinking that perhaps he shouldn't have blabbed in front of them.

Then he notices the newspapers scattered over the beds. He sees the headlines about me. He picks a paper up and reads it.

He looks amazed, but I can see he hasn't realised the awful truth yet.

How can I think about rescuing Jamal and Bibi when my own family is facing total disaster?

# CHAPTER TWENTY-FIVE

The time is approximately 2.35 a.m. and I'm proceeding in a northerly direction across the school cricket oval.

I stare up at the sky. Millions of stars

glitter like pearl earrings scattered on Mum's black floor tiles in the kitchen.

I think of the refugees in their desert prison. Perhaps they're looking up at the stars like me. Wondering, like me, if their misery will ever end.

I'm sorry, Jamal and Bibi.

I wanted to help you, I really did.

But now I have to go to Mum and Dad so they can yell at me for getting the family in the media and then I can help them pack up the house so we can move to another country.

We'll have to change our name again so nobody can track us down, not even our friends.

Maybe have plastic surgery.

Or at least wigs.

The stars are all blurry now. I wipe the tears away and concentrate on my escape plan. Dave the bodyguard can't patrol an entire school this size. I'll wait till the moon goes behind a cloud, then climb over the side fence.

'Bridget.'

I freeze.

Somebody just hissed my name.

I look around wildly for somewhere

to hide. That's the trouble with escaping across cricket pitches. No trees or long grass. There aren't even any kangaroos to duck behind.

I start running.

I can hear the thud of footsteps coming after me.

How did he know? How did Dave know I was going for the side fence? Must be the training. They must do a special course in side fences.

I glance over my shoulder to see how close he is. And stop. It's not Dave panting towards me out of the darkness.

'Menzies,' I say. 'What are you doing here?'

He doesn't say anything for a while, just pants. But I can tell from his face he's pretty upset. He must have guessed what I've decided to do.

Finally he manages to speak.

'Dave's gone,' he says.

'What do you mean, gone?' I say.

'He's been ordered back to Canberra,' says Menzies. 'I woke up when he slid a note under my door. By the time I got down to the carpark he was gone. That's when I saw you.'

I stare at Menzies, taking this in.

'And he didn't even say goodbye?' I whisper. Menzies looks at the ground.

'They never do, bodyguards,' he says sadly. 'It's the training.'

We look at each other in silence.

Part of me wishes I had bodyguard training too. It's really hard saying goodbye to your only friend. 'Where are you going?' says Menzies.

I've been dreading him asking, hoping I didn't have to say the words, wishing I could leave him a note as well.

I can't.

'Home,' I say. 'To start a new life somewhere else with Mum and Dad.'

Now I'm the one staring at the ground. I'm Menzies' only friend too. He'll be all alone in this place. I hate the thought of that.

We look at each other again.

'Thanks for being my friend,' I whisper. 'Sorry I didn't say goodbye before.'

Menzies doesn't say anything.

I try to think of something cheerful

to add. 'Now Dave's gone you'll be able to rescue Jamal and Bibi.'

I know it's stupid even before I finish saying it. Menzies stays silent for a bit. Then he shakes his head.

'One person can't do a rescue like that,' he says quietly. 'Not even if I was trained.'

I know. Now I feel even worse.

'I'm sorry,' I say. 'I wish I didn't have to leave. But I've got to go into hiding.'

Menzies takes a step towards me and for a moment I think he's going to grab me. He doesn't. He just pushes his glasses up his nose and looks at me, eyes big and worried.

'Bridget,' he says. 'What if your parents don't want you to go into hiding with them?'

I stare at him.

Suddenly I want to grab him. And shake him. But only because he might be right.

I've just exposed my family's guilty past to every newspaper and TV channel and talkback radio show in Australia. If I was Mum and Dad I'd be furious. Maybe so furious I wouldn't

153

even want me around.

Menzies is still looking at me, eyes big.

I realise what he's up to.

'I haven't got time to rescue refugees,' I hiss at him. 'I've just put my family in danger and I've got to find some way of rescuing them.'

'Exactly,' says Menzies. 'That's what I'm trying to say. Perhaps the best way you can help them isn't nicking off. Perhaps it's staying here at school and getting good marks and becoming a success in society and earning respect for your whole family.'

I stare at him for a long time, thinking about this.

Suddenly I want to hug him because he's right. And because he's my friend.

That's why Mum and Dad sent me to this school, to earn respect and admiration for our family. Suddenly it's all so clear.

Suddenly I feel so much better.

I just wish Menzies didn't look so sad.

# CHAPTER TWENTY-SIX

My guts are a bit wobbly as I walk across the courtyard towards the headmaster's office.

Partly it's tiredness because I've been awake most of the night planning my future career as a lawyer.

Partly it's anxiety because I've never apologised to a headmaster about my family before, and I'm not sure how good I'll be at it.

But mostly what's making my insides tremble is sadness.

I keep thinking about Jamal and Bibi.

I have to stop that.

I pause on the steps of the main building and look up at the school crest over the entrance. It's in Latin, but I know what it means.

Our Minds Are Open And Our Hearts Are Strong.

I have to be strong. In a few years when I'm giving a brilliant speech to a jury in the high court, and they're just about to agree that my client is allowed to knock down some cruddy old houses to build a really top-notch office block, I have to be strong enough not to think of Jamal and Bibi and start blubbing in front of everyone.

Instead I have to be strong in my heart and think about Mum and Dad. How proud they are of my success. How grateful they are for the admiration and respect I'm bringing to the name Podger or White or whatever we're calling ourselves at the time.

Our Minds Are Open And Our Hearts Are Strong.

I repeat this to myself several times as I go up the steps and into the building. It helps me stop thinking about Jamal and Bibi.

Almost.

I don't stop thinking about them completely until I look down the corridor past the genuine oil paintings and the genuine priceless porcelain vases and see who's sitting miserably on a genuine leather couch outside the headmaster's office.

Mum and Dad.

# CHAPTER TWENTY-SEVEN

Just as I reach Mum and Dad, the headmaster steps out of his office.

'Thank you for responding so promptly to my call, Mr and Mrs White,' says Mr Galbraith with a smile. 'Would you like to come into my office?'

Then he sees me.

'Oh,' he says. 'You have your daughter with you.' Mum and Dad look up, startled.

They didn't see me coming. I crept along the corridor quietly because I wanted to try and spot what mood they were in. Angry, or very angry. But both their faces are more sad than angry. Which makes me feel even worse.

'If we're going to talk about our daughter,' says Mum to Mr Galbraith, 'she should hear it as well.'

'Of course,' says Mr Galbraith.

As he ushers us into his office, I try to catch Mum or Dad's eye to let them know everything's going to be OK.

I don't manage to.

Mum, Dad and Mr Galbraith sit down. There isn't another chair so I stay standing.

'Well, Bridget,' says Mr Galbraith, smiling at me. 'I hear you had beautiful weather on your trip to Canberra.'

Before I can reply, he turns to Mum and Dad, who are looking a bit confused.

'Mr and Mrs White,' says Mr Galbraith. 'I'm going to come straight to the point. Your daughter's conduct in Canberra was commendable vis-à-vis the setting of personal goals, the planning of an outcome-oriented strategy, and the execution of a pre-determined agenda.'

Mum and Dad are looking very confused. I'm not surprised. Mr Galbraith sounds just like the Prime Minister.

'Regrettably, however,' continues Mr Galbraith, 'the dramatic nature of her conduct was not in keeping with this school's tradition of restraint and decorum. My colleagues on the school board have very real concerns that this school may not be the most suitable for Bridget's future development. It is felt, therefore, that in Bridget's best interests she be withdrawn from enrolment.'

'Eh?' says Dad.

'I don't understand,' says Mum.

Now that I'm learning the language important people speak, I do.

'I'm being expelled,' I whisper to Mum and Dad.

'Expelled?' gasps Mum.

'We prefer to say withdrawn,' says Mr Galbraith.

Desperately I open my mouth to tell him that I'm a reformed character. That I'm giving up trying to help refugees. That I'm aiming to be dux of the school and an eminent old girl.

Before I can, Dad stands up.

'Now just a sec,' he says. 'My daughter was in Canberra on a mission of mercy and compassion. And if my Latin serves me right, mercy and compassion happens to be the motto of this school.'

'Our Minds Are Open And Our Hearts Are Strong,' says Mr Galbraith.

'OK,' says Dad. 'I got it a bit wrong. But my daughter didn't get it wrong in wanting to help poor kids who are locked up. I'm proud of what Bridget did in Canberra.'

'Leonard,' says Mum quietly. 'Sit down.'

Dad stays standing.

I want to hug him right here in the headmaster's office. I don't care if hugging is against every rule in the school and I get a million detentions on my last day.

Before I can, Mr Galbraith stands up.

'We are proud of Bridget, too, Mr White,' he says. 'In a sense. But this school's mission statement is clear. We are charged with passing on the finest values and modes of behaviour to young people from the very best families. I'm sure you understand what I'm saying. We have the son of a government minister enrolled here.'

'I know,' says Dad. 'He was at my birthday party.'

Mr Galbraith stares at Dad for a moment. Then his eyes narrow slightly.

'I'm afraid the school board's decision is final, Mr White,' he says. 'If you'd like some counselling, we can refer you to an excellent grief therapist.'

Dad's eyes narrow too, which isn't a good sign. Dad doesn't lose his temper often, but when he does, watch out. He punched a Bulgarian toaster once when he found it was a cheap copy made in Latvia.

Mum stands up.

'Mr Galbraith,' she says. 'We chose this school because we wanted our daughter to have more than she could get from us. Now I happen to think she went too far in Canberra. But if you're telling us that her compassion is against the values of this school, then I think we're wasting our money.'

Mr Galbraith looks at Mum and Dad with an expression of sad regret.

'I fear you may have a very good point there, Mr and Mrs White,' he says. 'Have you considered a state school for Bridget? There are some very fine ones that would almost certainly give your daughter more than she could get from people like you and your husband.'

Now Mum's eyes narrow, which is a very bad sign. When her cousin Rooster got drunk in a nightclub once and insulted a woman, Mum went round to his place the next day and hit him with a chicken casserole.

I've got to do something.

Mum hitting Mr Galbraith will only make things worse.

Perhaps I should speak up now and tell everyone about my plan to be a successful corporate lawyer. Except I'm not sure if I want to be one any more.

Before I can think of anything else to say, a loud commotion outside in the corridor makes us all turn round.

The door bursts open. Mr Creely strides in. In front of him he's gripping a short man in a long shirt. Behind them both is Menzies, glasses crooked and face pink with alarm.

'Sorry to interrupt, Mr Headmaster,' says Mr Creely. 'I apprehended this man trying to break into the boys' building. I think he might be a terrorist.'

'He's Jamal's father,' says Menzies.

Mr Galbraith snatches up a phone. 'Miss Pryne,' he says. 'We have an intruder. Call the police and initiate the school's anti-terrorist plan.'

'He's not a terrorist,' I say. 'He's a dad.'

'Wait a sec, Bridget,' says Dad. He turns to Menzies. 'Is this bloke the dad of those kids in the detention centre?'

Menzies nods.

Jamal's father stops struggling in Mr Creely's grip and looks at Dad.

'You are Mr White?' he says. 'The father of Bridget? Menzies told me about you on the telephone.'

'The name's Podger,' says Dad. 'Len Podger. Dad of Bridget Podger. Pleased to meet you.'

'Mohammed Houssini,' says Jamal's father. He gives us all a hopeful smile. But even while he's smiling, he still looks tired and anxious.

Dad looks up at Mr Creely, who is still gripping Jamal's father by the arms.

'Let him go,' says Dad. 'He's with me.'

I can't believe it. My dad is more wonderful than I ever knew.

Mr Creely grips poor Jamal's father more tightly. Dad's eyes narrow. He reaches into his inside pocket and takes a step towards Mr Creely.

Mr Creely lets Jamal's father go and takes a nervous step backwards. Dad pulls out a Bulgarian gameboy and slaps it into Mr Creely's hand.

'Go and play Alien Invaders,' he says.

I feel like cheering. When I'm a refugee rights lawyer I'll tell this story at conferences.

'Mr and Mrs White,' says Mr Galbraith angrily. 'Please take your daughter out of here now and leave us to deal with this trespasser.'

'He's not a trespasser, sir,' says Menzies. 'I invited him.'

Mr Galbraith looks like he's going to expel Menzies as well. Before he can, Dad strides over to him.

'I've read letters written by this bloke's son,' says Dad to Mr Galbraith. 'This bloke risked everything for his kids, including his life. Take a long hard look at the parents at this school and tell me how many of them have done that.'

For a second Mr Galbraith doesn't know what to say. Then he thrusts his chin forward.

'Just what I'd expect,' he says. 'A criminal standing up for a criminal. Get out.'

Dad thrusts his chin right back at Mr Galbraith.

'Leonard,' says Mum sharply.

She steers Jamal's father towards the door and signals for the rest of us to follow. Mr Creely steps forward as if he's going to try and stop Jamal's father leaving. Dad glares at him and Mr Creely backs off.

'Come on,' says Dad to me and Menzies. 'Let's get out of here before I forget I'm a law-abiding citizen.'

On the way out I grab the Russian blender from the top of Mr Galbraith's filing cabinet.

He doesn't deserve it.

# CHAPTER TWENTY-EIGHT

We all walk down the corridor past the wood panels and the vases and the paintings, which don't look so genuine anymore.

Several of us are trembling. Me, for a start, and Menzies. Dad's hands are shaking a bit, though that might just be the stress of having a daughter who's exposed the family in the national media and been expelled in the same week.

Mum seems fairly relaxed. She's probably just pretending so Jamal's father feels he's in safe hands.

Jamal's father isn't trembling at all. He looks exhausted but calm. I guess when you've survived explosions and pirates and detention centres, a bossy headmaster isn't such a big deal.

As we leave the building, someone calls my name. It's Chantelle. She hurries over with Veuve and Antoinette.

'Bridget,' she says excitedly. 'I just

rang my dad. He reckons if you graduate in law from uni with first class honours and don't get arrested again, he'll give you a job in our law firm.'

'Thanks,' I say.

I decide not to go into my new career plan right now. But I do have a thought.

'Does your dad take refugee cases?' I ask her. Chantelle notices Jamal's father for the first time. She looks at him doubtfully.

'I think we're a bit tied up in court at the moment,' she says. 'We're suing a construction company.'

'What about you, Menzies,' says Antoinette. 'Why doesn't your dad help the refugees? Or is he too busy spending our taxes on overseas trips?' Menzies looks hurt but doesn't say anything.

Jamal's father puts his hand on Menzies' shoulder. 'It's OK, Menzies, I understand,' he says softly. 'Your father is a politician, and politicians must do what is right for politics. It is the same in my country.'

'In Australia,' mutters Dad, 'we

prefer them just to do what's right.'

Jamal's father turns to him.

'Mr Podger,' he says. 'Will you help my family?'

Dad, who was about to express some more thoughts about politicians, suddenly doesn't know what to say.

'I ask you,' says Jamal's father, 'because you are a powerful man. Menzies told me you are an importer of goods. In Afghanistan, importers are wealthy and powerful men too. I beg you, Mr Podger, as an important and respected citizen, please help us.'

Dad is lost for words. So is Mum.

'My son and daughter are good children,' continues Jamal's father. 'They try to give presents to the guards, they try to play soccer with them, and Jamal once tried to bake bread for their morning tea using only flour and grass seeds. But I fear for them. Bibi has tooth pain, and I fear Jamal is planning something dangerous.'

Jamal's father pauses, his dark eyes clouded with worry.

I wonder if I should tell him what Jamal is planning. I decide not to. No point worrying him more.

'There is something worse, Mr Podger,' says Jamal's father. 'I am worried Jamal and Bibi and my wife will be sent back to Afghanistan without me. My country is in chaos. Warlords rule. They are from a different tribal group and they hate my people. If they could, they would kill my family.'

I stare in horror at Jamal's father. This is even worse than toothache and plastic pipes in the guts.

Jamal's father grips Dad's arm.

'You are a father too, Mr Podger. I know you would die for your family like me. But I fear my life is not enough. Please, help my children.'

Jamal's father looks at Dad with so much dignity mixed up with helplessness that I want to cry.

I can see Dad is feeling moved as well. I can also see what he's thinking.

*I've got a son in jail too. I can't even help my own son.*

Dad looks at Mum.

I know what she's thinking as well.

*Our family. We have to look after our*

*family first.*

But I'm wrong because Mum does an amazing thing. She nods at Dad.

Dad looks at us all for a moment, frowning. He turns and looks back at Mr Galbraith, who's standing in the doorway of his building glaring at us.

'OK,' says Dad quietly. 'Let's see if we can get those kids out of that place.'


## CHAPTER TWENTY-NINE

When Dad does a job, he moves fast. We only left the school a few hours ago and already we've picked up stuff from the warehouse, visited Gavin in jail, bought food and drink for the trip, dropped Mum off at home, and now me and Menzies are sitting in Dad's car outside Uncle Grub's place.

I was hoping Mum would be coming on the job with us, but I know why she can't. When you do a job you have to make sure you haven't got any illegal stuff at home in case you get arrested and the police search under your beds.

Right now Mum's clearing out all the Iraqi pressure cookers and US army toothbrushes and taking them to the warehouse.

Menzies leans over from the back seat.

'What's taking your dad so long?' he says. 'Jamal could be on his way to Afghanistan while we're sitting here.'

I sigh. This is about the tenth time Menzies has said this since Dad took Jamal's father into Uncle Grub's place only about fifteen minutes ago.

'I've told you,' I say. 'They're planning the job. If you try and do a job without a plan, you're history. Uncle Ray told me once how he had to patch up three blokes who tried to do a jail break without a proper plan. They tunnelled into a pet shop by mistake.'

Menzies doesn't look convinced.

'Surely it doesn't take this long to do a plan,' he says.

'A job like this it does,' I say. 'There's the tunnel to think about, spades, pickaxes, ropes, planks of wood, torches, possibly explosives, plus disguises, a getaway route, heaps of stuff. They're probably ringing Uncle Ray for first aid advice in case any of us gets hurt.'

I wish I hadn't said that. Menzies is looking alarmed and suddenly I'm feeling a bit nervous too.

'Don't worry,' I say to Menzies, and to myself. 'Dad's a professional.'

Menzies still looks worried.

'How are we going to fit all the tunnelling stuff into one car?' he says.

'We're not,' I say. 'Uncle Grub'll bring his van. One of the rules for doing a job is never put all your eggs in the one vehicle.'

Menzies looks impressed at this piece of criminal wisdom. I decide not to tell him I got it from *The Bill* on TV.

Even though Menzies is a worrier, I'm glad he's coming on the job. Mum and Dad were doubtful about taking him out of school, but Jamal's father insisted and as it turned out nobody noticed. Everybody was too busy hiding in the library cellar after the anti-terrorist bell went off.

'At last,' says Menzies.

Dad and Jamal's father are heading

out of Uncle Grub's place and coming towards the car. Dad's got a fistful of Uncle Grub's maps.

'OK,' says Dad as they get in. 'We're set. The detention centre's a fair old distance away so we'll be driving through the night. Anyone got a problem with that?'

We all shake our heads.

Jamal's father's eyes are shining and I can see that driving through the night in an ancient Mercedes with squeaky shock absorbers to rescue his kids is the thing he wants to do most in the whole world.

He reaches out and puts his hand on Dad's shoulder.

'Before we start,' he says, 'I want to say, my heart is full with your kindness.'

Dad puts his hand on Jamal's father's arm. 'You're very welcome, Mohammed,' he says. 'But don't be too grateful till we see how we go.'

173

# CHAPTER THIRTY

We've been on the road for hours.

Dad's having to do all the driving. Jamal's father offered to help, but Dad said no. Jamal's father is a taxi driver and in Afghanistan he's probably driven about two hundred thousand k's further than Dad in his life, but he doesn't have an Australian driving licence. Dad reckons it'd be too risky. If we got pulled over with Jamal's father driving, the whole job would be down the dunny.

Menzies offered too. He drives a ute on his uncle's farm. Dad said the same to him.

Menzies and Jamal's father are asleep in the back, Menzies' head on Jamal's father's shoulder.

I've been staring out into the darkness for ages, thinking. And keeping an eye out for kangaroos on the road like Dad asked me to.

There's heaps of stuff I want to ask him about the job.

How are we going to get to the dentention centre fence without being seen?

Are we going to use explosives in the tunnel and if so how are we going to do it without the guards hearing us?

How far behind us is Uncle Grub in his van? Uncle Grub's a really fast driver and I'm surprised he hasn't overtaken us yet.

I haven't asked Dad any of these things. If he wanted me to know he would have told me. I saw the same thing on *The Bill.* Junior members of a gang never get told the whole plan in case they get arrested and interrogated.

There is one thing I have to ask, though. I glance across at Dad.

In the light from the dash I can see his face is set and his thoughts are miles away. Probably in the same place as mine.

'Dad,' I say.

'Yeah?' he says.

'There's something bothering me,' I say.

'What's that?' he says.

Instead of trying to get Jamal and

Bibi out,' I say, 'shouldn't we be trying to get Gavin out?' Dad thinks about this, but not for long.

'No,' he says softly. 'With Gavin it was a fair cop and he deserves to be inside. These kids don't.' Dad glances across at me and I can see he's as sad about Gavin as I am.

But I'm glad that was his answer.

## CHAPTER THIRTY-ONE

This desert road is so straight.

Dad hasn't turned the wheel for ages. Not a curve, not a twist. Just two straight headlight beams stabbing into the darkness.

I wish my thoughts would stay as straight as the road.

Get to the detention centre, do the job, free Jamal and Bibi and their mother.

Straightforward.

But my thoughts keep curving and twisting all over the place.

Did I kiss Mum goodbye?

Should we be bringing bullet-proof vests?

And no matter where they twist and curve, my thoughts keep coming back to the stuff Gavin told me when we saw him yesterday.

As usual Mum and Dad gave me some time alone with him in the prison visiting room. I wasn't going to tell him about the job, but once it was just me and him I couldn't stop myself.

Because he's a top-notch big brother, he was very kind.

'Go for it, Bridge,' he said. 'If anyone can do it, you and Dad can. Just try and keep your nose clean.'

But then he told me about a couple of blokes in his section who escaped once. They were recaptured after only three days, and they reckoned those were the worst three days of their lives.

'I'm not surprised,' I said to Gavin. 'Hiding in an empty offal tank in a pet food factory.'

'That's not my point,' said Gavin. 'My point is that most people can't stand the stress and fear. For most people, being on the run is even worse than being inside.'

At the time I told Gavin I reckoned it was still worth getting Jamal and Bibi and their mother out, so we could get Bibi to a dentist and stop them all being sent back to the warlords.

But now I'm thinking about it, I don't want them to have to spend the rest of their lives on the run suffering from stress and fear.

So I hope Dad's plan covers what's going to happen after we've done the job.


# CHAPTER THIRTY-TWO

I wake up.

My neck is stiff and my eyes hurt in the bright desert sunlight and I've got the seatbelt strap stuck to my face.

'Are we there yet?' I say.

Dad doesn't reply.

That's because he's not in the car.

'Dad?' I say, alarmed.

The engine is still running, but we're parked in a big dusty carpark. For a second I hope it's the carpark of somewhere that sells pies and milkshakes because I'm really hungry and thirsty. Plus that would explain where Dad is.

But it's not.

Outside the car window I can see a high chook-wire fence and behind it drab dusty buildings with no signs advertising pies or anything.

The fence has got razor wire on top.

Suddenly I'm wide awake.

I realise where we are.

We're parked outside the refugee detention centre. I squint anxiously across the carpark. We're in full view of the guards. There's a military-type checkpoint only about fifty metres from the car.

What is Dad thinking of?

In a panic I turn to the back seat.

'Where's Dad?' I say.

Menzies is still waking up, rubbing his eyes and looking confused.

Jamal's father isn't there either.

I get out of the car. A blast of hot air hits me like a Latvian hairdryer on perm. I squint around, looking for

Dad. The flat desert horizon shimmers in the heat. The detention centre fence hums mournfully in the hot wind. We're the only car in the carpark. I can't see Dad anywhere.

I have a wild hopeful thought.

Perhaps Dad has parked here as a decoy while he and Jamal's father and Uncle Grub tunnel in round the back.

Then, over the rumble of the car engine, I hear Dad whistling. Not the soft urgent whistle people use when they're doing a job. *Jailbreak* by AC/DC.

The car boot is up and I see a flash of blue cloth behind it. I go round to the back of the car.

Dad is standing on one foot taking his jeans off. He's wearing a yellow shirt and the jacket of his blue suit, and the suit pants are flapping on a hanger dangling from the boot catch.

Jamal's father is holding Dad's arm so Dad doesn't fall over.

'What are you doing?' I say to Dad.

'G'day love,' he says. 'Getting my good gear on. Can't talk to the management of a detention centre looking like a scruff.'

I stare at him, stunned.

'Talk to the management?' I say.

'Tell 'em what they're doing to those kids is against the law,' says Dad. 'Uncle Grub rang a lawyer he knows. Locking kids up like this is breaking about three different parts of the Child Protection Act.'

'This is a good law,' says Jamal's father. 'We will use it to free my family.'

I gawk at Dad as he zips up his suit pants. 'You're just going to walk in through the front gate?' I say. 'In broad daylight?'

Dad looks at me with a puzzled expression. 'Yes,' he says. 'What did you think I was going to do? Dig a tunnel in the dead of night?'

I feel faint.

'So,' I croak, 'Uncle Grub isn't coming?'

Dad shakes his head while he slips his good shoes on. 'I thought it'd be best if he didn't. George is top-notch when it comes to, you know, doing a job. But he's a bit rough round the edges for a meeting with management.'

My head is buzzing and not just from the sun. 'I think it'll be best if just me and Mr Houssini go in,' says Dad. 'I'll leave the car running so you and Menzies have got air-conditioning.'

I get back in the car.

I don't know what else to do.

One glance at Menzies' face and I can tell he heard what me and Dad were just saying.

I stare over at the detention centre, trying to see if I can spot anyone behind the fence. Through the dust and glare I can just make out a few people moving between the buildings. I can't tell if they're refugees or guards.

I look away.

Dad slams the boot.

'Wish us luck,' he yells, waving at me and Menzies through the window.

I wave back, but I can hardly move my arm.

'Perhaps they'll pull it off,' says Menzies as we watch them walk over to the checkpoint. 'Perhaps this way'll work.'

I don't reply.

No point.

In about five seconds Dad and Jamal's father will be turned away from the checkpoint, possibly after being bashed up.

I can hardly watch. But I do because if the guards try to hurt my dad I'll go over there and use Uncle Ray's finger jabs.

'Look,' says Menzies. 'It's working.'

At first I don't know what he means.

Then I do.

This is amazing.

The guards are letting them through. They're escorting Dad and Jamal's father to the main gate. Another guard at the main gate is making a phone call. The main gate is opening. Dad and Jamal's father are going in.

'Yes,' says Menzies.

'Yes,' I yell.

It's working.

# CHAPTER THIRTY-THREE

It didn't work.

I can tell it didn't from the slump in Dad's shoulders and the way Jamal's father is shouting angrily. And the fact that both of them are being escorted back to the checkpoint by four guards who are pushing them.

Me and Menzies stare at each other helplessly. It was looking so good.

Dad and Jamal's father were inside one of the detention centre buildings for almost ten minutes. As each minute passed, Menzies and I got more and more excited. We'd just decided that Jamal and Bibi should enrol in my old school with me, when suddenly Dad and Jamal's father reappeared, shouting and being pushed.

'Oh no,' groaned Menzies.

The guards are still pushing them now.

Jamal's father tries to run back through the gate. The guards stop him.

I get out of the car.

I want to fling myself at the fence and tear it down and let all the kids run free into the desert.

I don't care about the guards or the razor wire or how upset the Prime Minister will be.

Suddenly I see a car speeding towards us across the carpark. It stops next to ours. From the logo on the side I can tell it's a TV news car.

A man and a woman get out.

The man has a camera and the woman has a microphone, both pointing at me.

'Hey, parliament house girl,' says the woman. 'What are you doing here?'

For a second I think about telling them to rack off and stop pestering me and my family. Then I realise perhaps I can say something that will help Jamal and Bibi.

There's so much to say I hardly know where to start.

'There are kids locked up in there,' I say to the camera. 'Kids who haven't done anything wrong. They haven't burgled anyone or shoplifted anything or even thought about robbing a bank.'

This probably isn't the best way for me to be saying this.

I remember the letter from Jamal I was reading in the car on the way back from Canberra. I brought it on this trip in case I got scared and needed inspiration.

'This is a letter from one of those kids,' I say.

I pull it out of my pocket and start reading it to the camera.

*'I have bad news. My father is free . . .'*

I read the whole letter.

When I get to the end, the bit about how Jamal is sad because he thought Australia was a kind place, I see the cameraman glance at the reporter. She signals to him to keep filming.

I look right into the camera.

'I met the Prime Minister last week,' I say. 'He said these kids are being locked up for us, the people of Australia. We're only four people, but we're here because we don't want any kids to suffer for us. My dad reckons that's how all Australians used to feel. I wish they still did.'

I stop.

The guards have seen the camera and they're running towards us, yelling.

Anyway, there's no point saying more.

I look around at the fence and the guards and the checkpoint and the razor wire.

Words won't help Jamal and Bibi now.

Only me and Menzies can do that.


## CHAPTER THIRTY-FOUR

I strain my ears to hear what sort of breathing sounds are coming from the other bedroom.

Lucky these motels have got thin walls. I can hear a low rumble coming from Dad and a soft wheeze coming from Jamal's father.

'They're asleep,' I whisper to Menzies.

We both get out of our beds as quietly as we can and put our shoes on. It was hot in bed wearing all my clothes, but I did it to save time.

187

'Towels,' I whisper to Menzies.

'Getting them,' he whispers.

While he creeps into the bathroom, I feel around on the floor for our water bottles. It's not easy, getting the equipment for a job together in total darkness, but we can't risk switching the lights on.

'Got the towels,' whispers Menzies in my ear.

I've got the water bottles. And the chocolate and lollies and horse photos that Antoinette, Chantelle and Veuve gave us for Jamal and Bibi.

We tiptoe to the door, open it carefully so the chain doesn't rattle, slip out and close it behind us as quietly as we can.

There's a bit of moonlight so we can see our way past the parked cars of the other guests.

Suddenly Menzies grabs me.

'We haven't got anything to dig with,' he says.

'Relax,' I say. 'This is a motel. They've got to have gardening equipment around here somewhere.'

We start hunting.

Nothing. Not even a crowbar for giving their septic tank a prod.

'This is hopeless,' says Menzies. 'How can we tunnel into a detention centre without gardening equipment?'

Just as he says this, I see two spades strapped to the back of a four wheel drive outside one of the motel units. I go over and carefully unstrap them.

They're compact metal camping spades, solid and sturdy. I lift one down and see the words stamped into the back of it.

Made In Bulgaria.

Menzies has grabbed two more spades strapped to the same vehicle. They're small and plastic. 'The more the better,' he says.

He takes two small plastic buckets as well.

I don't feel good, stealing other kids' beach toys, so I reach into my sock and pull out the emergency ten dollars Dad gave me before we left home.

'Have you got any money?' I ask Menzies.

'Only fifty dollars,' he says.

I leave the sixty dollars tucked

behind the spare wheel. Even though what we're about to do will involve breaking about eighteen laws, that's still no reason to be dishonest.

## CHAPTER THIRTY-FIVE

The road to the detention centre is very flat and very straight and luckily there are no cars.

This time my thoughts are straight too.

Get there, do the job, free Jamal and Bibi and their mum.

The road to the detention centre is also very long.

'It'll be light by the time we get there,' says Menzies. 'My feet hurt already.'

'It's about a four hour walk,' I say. 'I measured it in the car while we were driving to the motel this afternoon. That means once we get to the fence we'll have another four hours for digging before it gets light.'

Menzies sighs.

'I still think we should have brought Jamal's father,' he says.

'I don't like leaving him either,' I say. 'But he was too upset. I'm not surprised. To be in a detention centre for nearly ten minutes and not be allowed to see your kids. What a mongrel act. But if someone's too upset, they can't come on a job. It's the rule.'

I don't tell Menzies it's a rule I've just made up.

It's based on fact. Every time on *The Bill* someone goes on a job emotionally upset, they get arrested.

'Arghhh,' yells Menzies. 'What's that?'

'It's a lizard,' I say. 'It won't hurt you. Remember Mr Lamb told us about them in geography? They burrow into the desert sand.'

'Hop it, lizard,' says Menzies, waving his buckets and spades. 'You'll only get jealous when you see how good we are at digging.'

We walk on.

I stare up at the sky.

The stars in the desert are so much

brighter than I've ever seen before. When I was little, Dad told me that every star is a human wish. If that's true, with so many of them directly above us we must be getting close to the detention centre.

## CHAPTER THIRTY-SIX

The detention centre looks huge at night.

Must be because it's all lit up and the desert around it is dark.

Menzies and me crouch behind a spindly bush at the very edge of the darkness and peer across at the compound. I can't see any guards, but who knows how many security cameras they've got disguised as rocks.

I reckon it's about fifty metres to the fence. That's the next part of the job. To get across that lit-up dirt without being spotted.

'It's a long way,' says Menzies.

'Could be worse,' I say. 'Imagine if the motel towels were blue.'

Menzies smiles, which is pretty good for a kid whose feet have been bleeding for the last hour. When this job is over I'm going to get him a decent pair of Hungarian elastic-sided boots instead of those shoddily-made three hundred dollar American things he's wearing.

Menzies lies face-down on the ground, spades gripped in one hand, buckets in the other, water bottle stuck in the back of his belt.

I drape one of the towels over him so no part of his body is visible.

It's a pretty good match. The orangy ochre colour of the towel is almost the same as the colour of the desert dirt. He's so well camouflaged he could almost be a lizard.

I lie down and drag the other towel over me. We set off, crawling on our tummies, staying under our towels.

'Ow,' says Menzies after about two seconds. 'These stones are sharp.'

'Shhh,' I whisper. 'Sound travels further at night in the desert.'

When Uncle Grub was burgling he always kept very quiet near sandpits for just that reason.

As we wriggle painfully towards the detention centre fence, Menzies doesn't speak again, just swears softly to himself.

I don't blame him. As well as sharp stones there are little tufts of grass with thorns in them. And ants that bite. And I have to pinch my nose every few metres to stop myself sneezing from the dust.

I don't even want to think about snakes.

After a long time I peek out from under my towel.

The fence is only about two metres away.

'Far enough,' I whisper to Menzies.

He looks out from under his towel.

'The closer we get the less we have to dig,' he says, and slithers on.

'And the more we can be seen,' I say.

Menzies stops.

We wriggle close to each other so our towels meet up and we can make a little tent out of them. I start scraping at the ground with my metal spade. The dirt is hard and crusty here. Must have got squashed a bit when they built the fence.

Menzies starts scraping too.

'Gently,' I whisper. 'No big movements till we've got a hole big enough to hide in.'

Slowly we slide each spadeful of dirt out from under our towels.

I try to imagine what we'd look like to any guard who comes out the back for a pee and spots us. Like two lizards, I hope.

Two lizards trying to do the right thing.


## CHAPTER THIRTY-SEVEN

My arms ache so much I want to cry.

But I don't care.

We've done it.

We've dug a hole big enough for us both to climb down into. Bigger, in fact, because once we scraped through the desert crust, we found the dirt down here is softer.

Now we can start the real tunnelling.

I take a deep breath and send a

silent prayer to my ancestor Benedict Podger.

*Give my arms strength. Let me be as good at this as you were.*

'My arms are seizing up,' moans Menzies.

'Keep going,' I urge him. 'Think of Jamal and Bibi.'

I've been thinking of them for hours. Hoping they're not on a plane to Afghanistan with plastic tubes down their throats.

I've been thinking about something else too. Now that our hole is too big to camouflage with towels, I'm worried we might be seen. Out in this flat country our piles of dirt must look like mini mountains.

I pray none of the guards needs a pee.

If only they all had Bulgarian gameboys to keep them occupied.

Trouble is, they don't.

I know because suddenly I can hear footsteps crunching across the dry ground. More than one person by the sound of them.

Coming closer.

In the gloom I see the whites of Menzies' eyes get bigger. I put my hand over his mouth to stop him doing any loud gasps.

We cower in the mouth of the tunnel we've started.

The tunnel we may never get to finish.

Menzies grips me tight.

Then I gasp.

Faintly silhouetted against the starry sky is a head and shoulders peering down into our hole. It's over.

We've failed.

We tried, Jamal and Bibi, we really did.

'Bridget,' hisses a voice. 'Have you gone dopey? What are you doing?'

Dad?

Sometimes surprise can rock your guts even more than fear. Right now my guts are nine on the Richter scale.

Dad doesn't wait for me to reply. I hear him hissing to somebody else.

'Quick, Mohammed, there's a light gone on in that building. Take cover.'

Suddenly the hole is full of falling dirt and bodies. Dad's armpit is over my face, I can tell it's him by the Bosnian deodorant. Menzies sounds like he's been squashed too, and I can hear Jamal's father whispering apologies.

After a lot of wriggling and groaning, we all get untangled.

The hole's just big enough for the four of us to crouch in a huddle.

'Of all the harebrained crazy schemes,' says Dad, glaring at me. 'This takes the Bulgarian biscuit. Do you realise what you could get for this? More years inside than I've got left. We all could.'

Normally I'd be crushed. When Dad gets depressed our whole family does. But this time I'm thinking of Jamal and Bibi.

'Only if we get caught,' I say. 'Come on, there's more of us to dig now.'

'No,' says Dad. 'Out of the question. We're getting you kids out of here.'

He grabs me and Menzies and starts to stand up. Then he stops and stares.

We all do.

Jamal's father has grabbed one of the spades and is digging like a maniac.

I've never seen a spade move so fast. Dirt is flying everywhere.

Dad pulls me and Menzies away, but he turns back.

Even in the gloom I can tell from his face what he's thinking.

This isn't just a harebrained crazy kid scheme any more.

This is a father trying to rescue his children.


## CHAPTER THIRTY-EIGHT

We've run out of time.

Even down here in the hole, with heaps of dirt half-blocking my view, I can see the pink creeping into the sky.

Dawn.

It'll be light soon and then the guards'll see us and we'll be arrested.

For a couple of hours I thought we were going to make it. We had a great excavation system going. Jamal's father digging, me and Menzies passing buckets of dirt along the tunnel, Dad chucking them out of the hole.

Every half hour we'd stop and have a square each of Antoinette's chocolate. I knew she wouldn't mind and Jamal's father said Jamal and Bibi wouldn't either.

Then Jamal's father hit concrete.

I still don't believe it.

What is concrete doing under the desert?

'Must be some sort of drainage pipe,' says Dad. 'Or sewer or something.'

We all stare at it.

I wish I could blow it up.

Dad kneels down and brushes dirt off the curved concrete surface of the pipe. Then he gets out his keys and has a scratch at it.

I admire his determination, but we just don't have the three weeks it'll take Dad to scratch his way through.

Dad starts stabbing the pipe with his keys. He's gone mental.

Hang on, no he hasn't.

The concrete's starting to crumble.

'This isn't concrete,' says Dad. 'This is very cheap and very nasty Albanian army cement. I was offered two hundred tonnes of it and I said no.

Looks like one of the sub-contractors on this place said yes.'

We all throw ourselves on our backs and start pounding the cement pipe with our feet. Chunks are caving in now. Soon there's a jagged gap big enough to climb through.

We peer in.

My chest lurches with excitement.

A little way down the pipeline, daylight is spilling in from above through what looks like a metal grating.

I do a quick calculation. Yes. The pipeline is proceeding in a northerly direction. It runs under the fence. The grating is inside the detention centre.

'Quick,' I say. 'We might just have time. If we crawl along the pipe and shift that grating and find Jamal and Bibi before the guards see us, we can get them out of here.'

Dad grabs hold of me.

'Bridget,' he says. 'It was a great try, but we can't do this in daylight. We have to go.'

'No,' I say. 'We can't leave Jamal and Bibi.'

'I know how you feel, love,' says Dad, and I can see he does. 'But we just have to hope they can hang on until enough Australians have a stern word with the government.'

Dad is still holding my arm. I pull myself free. 'What if they can't hang on?' I say.

Dad hesitates and I know he's thinking about all the practical things that could go wrong in the next few minutes. That's what dads do, its their job.

Dads who aren't desperate, that is.

Jamal's dad isn't standing around worrying. He's inside the pipe already, heading for the grating.

'Come on: I say to Dad and Menzies. 'We've got to help him.'

Then I realise Dad isn't thinking, he's listening. And now I hear it too.

A vehicle, coming towards us.

'Mohammed,' yells Dad. 'Get out of there.'

'Save yourselves,' shouts Jamal's dad. 'I have to be with my family.'

I don't stop to think either. I scramble out of the tunnel and fling myself at the edge of the hole, trying to drag myself out. If I can slow these guards down even for a couple of minutes, Jamal's dad might have a chance to get through the grating and be with his kids.

The edge of the hole is too crumbly. I can't get a proper grip to climb out.

A car door slams.

Suddenly I stop trying to get out of the hole. Astonishment turns my insides into soggy Albanian cement.

A face is peering down at me over the edge of the hole.

It's Dave the bodyguard.


## CHAPTER THIRTY-NINE

'Dave,' I gasp. 'What are you doing here?'

Dave doesn't seem to want to look at me. If my eyes hadn't just gone wobbly with tiredness and stress, I'd swear he was embarrassed. Except highly trained federal policemen don't get embarrassed.

Somebody else appears next to Dave, peering down into the hole.

Menzies' father, wearing a t-shirt.

Now I know I'm not seeing clearly. Except it is him. I'd recognise his voice anywhere.

'Menzies,' he calls anxiously. 'Are you all right?'

Dad and Menzies appear at my side.

'Dad,' squeaks Menzies.

'Oh, poop,' says Dad.

Menzies' father and Dave give us a hand to climb out of the hole. When we've scrambled out, we crouch with them behind a pile of dirt.

'Look,' says Dad. 'I'm sorry we didn't tell you we were bringing Menzies with us, but I can explain.'

'No you can't,' says Menzies' father. 'You haven't got a clue what's really going on here.'

Dad looks at him, uncertain.

'What do you mean?' I say.

'You tell them,' says Menzies' father to Dave. 'Seeing as you were part of it.'

Forget the training, Dave looks more miserable and embarrassed than anyone I've ever seen in my life, including Gavin at his first court appearance.

'You know that project on parasites you kids did at school,' mumbles Dave. 'Well, politicians are a bit like that, dependent on other organisms. They're called voters.'

He gives an apologetic glance at Menzies' father.

'Get to the point, Dave,' sighs Menzies' father.

'Certain people in the government,' says Dave, 'reckon they've found a way to get all our votes. By making us voters think they know how to keep us safe from terrorists.'

Dave pauses. I can see he really doesn't want to say the next bit. But he does.

'You're the terrorists.'

I can't believe what I'm hearing.

'Terrorists?' explodes Dad. 'We're not terrorists.'

'Of course not,' says Menzies' father. 'But you're a convicted criminal breaking into a high-security detention centre with an immigrant from a Muslim country. That makes you the

205

next best thing.'

The Albanian cement in my guts is turning hard and cold and I can't stop shivering.

What have I done?

If Dad's arrested as a terrorist he'll spend the rest of his life in jail.

'Dave,' says Menzies. 'What does my dad mean, you're a part of this?'

Dave looks away and doesn't answer.

'He was just keeping an eye on you,' says Menzies' father. 'Letting the government know what you were up to.'

Menzies looks like someone has whacked him with a spade.

'We should have had a Russian blender on really loud when we were planning this job,' says Menzies bitterly. 'And I should have guessed you hadn't really gone back to Canberra.'

'Menzies,' says his father. 'Dave was just doing his job.'

'Not any more,' mutters Dave. 'I've quit.'

Menzies stares at Dave, taking this in.

'Wait a minute,' says Dad to

Menzies' father. 'You're part of the government. You're in on this.'

'No I'm not,' sighs Menzies' father. 'Why would I be part of a plot to get my own son arrested?'

Dad thinks about this.

'Fair enough,' he says.

'We're telling the truth,' says Dave. 'Why do you think you haven't been arrested before now? You've got an open-cut mine here that can be seen from the moon. Because they want you inside the fence before they nab you, that's why. It's more dramatic. There's a SWAT team in there that's been monitoring every spadeful.'

Dad is looking as sick as I feel.

Menzies' father sticks his face close to Dad's. 'You dragged my son into this,' he says. 'All I care about is getting him out safely.'

Dad looks like he's close to tears. But he doesn't turn away from Menzies' father.

'I'm sorry,' says Dad.

'I want more than sorry,' says Menzies' father. 'When you're arrested in a few minutes, I want you to explain to the authorities that my son had nothing to do with this.'

'But I did,' says Menzies.

His father gives him a glare that would shatter even high-quality Bulgarian concrete.

Menzies doesn't flinch.

He just looks at his father, then gives him a hug.

'Is there any point,' says Dad, 'in all of us getting into Dave's car and driving very fast?'

Dave and Menzies' father shake their heads. Dad nods slowly and puts his arms round me.

I can see he knows he's going to jail for a very long time.

In the distance I can hear the sound of vehicles roaring towards us across the desert. Police cars, probably, and troop carriers and armoured personnel vehicles and tanks.

'I love you, Dad,' I whisper. 'I'll never forget what you tried to do for Jamal and Bibi.'

Dad hugs me tight.

I struggle not to cry in case this is the last time Dad sees me for a long time. I want him to remember me as a proud daughter.

Then I remember Jamal's dad.

I crouch and peer down into the tunnel. I can see him in the pipe, still struggling to shift the grating.

He's not going to get to his family in time.

I turn to the approaching vehicles, silently begging them to take a few more minutes to arrive. They don't.

They come into view almost immediately, and for a brief crazy moment I think I really am seeing things.

## CHAPTER FORTY

This is incredible.

Unbelievable.

I'm so excited, I'm almost Bulgarian jelly.

The vehicles roaring towards us across the desert aren't troop carriers and tanks, and mostly not police cars. They're ordinary cars and campervans and utes and buses and minibuses and motorbikes.

Hundreds of them.

And they're not full of SWAT teams and anti-terrorist units, or police, apart from the few dazed-looking officers in the few outnumbered police cars.

Most of the vehicles are packed with ordinary members of the Australian public, waving and shouting at us.

'Hey, parliament house girl,' yells an old lady from the window of a bus full of old ladies. 'Saw you on telly, love. You've got us off our bums.'

Menzies' eyes are almost bigger than his glasses.

Dad's eyes are pretty big too.

Menzies' father and Dave obviously weren't expecting this either.

'Incredible,' croaks Menzies' father. 'The power of a child's voice and a nation's conscience.'

'And telly,' says Dave.

People are jumping out of their vehicles and heading for our hole.

'Leave it to us,' says an old bloke with medals on his bowling club shirt. 'My mates didn't die fighting for an

Australia that locks up kiddies.'

'Too right,' says a woman pushing a baby in a stroller. 'I've been fretting about this whole business since it started, but now I've had a gutful.' Her friends, all pushing strollers as well, agree in loud voices.

A bunch of blokes who look like builders' labourers are digging with big spades, widening our hole so people can walk down into it more easily.

'You must be Bridget,' says a voice behind me.

I turn round. An elegantly dressed elderly woman is smiling at me. A uniformed chauffeur is supporting her elbow and holding a large picnic basket.

'I'm Chantelle's nana,' says the woman. She smiles at Menzies as well. 'I just want to say how pleased I am that Chantelle has made such admirable friends.'

She gives Menzies' father a sharp stare, then gives us all a little wave and joins the queue waiting to get along the tunnel and into the pipe.

Over the bobbing heads of all the

people crawling through the pipe, I can just make out a couple of burly blokes in singlets up front removing the grating.

They help Jamal's father up into the detention centre, then stay there, ready to lift the people in the tunnel and their eskies up after him. Or the people in the detention centre down into the tunnel.

I hold my breath.

Through the fence I can see a crowd of refugees, men and women and children, hurrying towards the edge of the empty grating hole.

I can also see uniformed officers pouring out of the buildings.

I remember what Gavin told me about the dangers of trying to escape and the misery of life on the run.

The uniformed officers all have weapons. I can hardly look.

But the refugees don't try to leave the detention centre.

They stand watching, smiling with amazement and delight as we go in and embrace them.

# CHAPTER FORTY-ONE

Several of the journalists here have told me that nothing like this has ever happened inside an Australian detention centre before.

I can believe it.

There probably hasn't been this much hugging anywhere in Australia before.

And nobody's been arrested, including us. The government must have decided that with so much media here, and so many voters, mass violence and arrests wouldn't look so good.

Dad's helped a lot. Handing out battery-operated Bulgarian personal massagers to the officers as well as the refugees has really helped keep the atmosphere light and friendly.

Menzies' dad is really impressed. He's planning to resign from the government and stand as an independent at the next election and I think he wants Dad to help him. He was saying just now that seeing all these ordinary Australians hugging and laughing with refugees gives him some really good clues about how a lot of people are going to vote.

Me and Menzies finally met Jamal and Bibi.

It was really emotional. I'd never seen a photo of them, and yet I knew it was them as soon as I saw them. I think it was the way Jamal was balancing a plastic bag soccer ball on his head and the way Bibi threw her arms round me and knocked me over.

It was Jamal's eyes as well.

I've never seen eyes that sparkle as much as his. For the rest of my life, whenever things get tough, I'll remember that it's technically possible to stay hopeful no matter what.

Bibi's sparkle a fair bit too, specially now Menzies' dad has told her he'll get her toothache fixed up quick smart. He's still a member of parliament, so he can arrange an x-ray on humanitarian grounds.

And a hip specialist for Jamal.

Me and Menzies have just played

soccer with Jamal and Bibi. They hadn't started their hunger strike, so apart from Jamal's limp they were both at match fitness.

They beat us eighteen nil, even though Menzies asked Dave to play on our side. We don't mind because they taught us some great ball tricks.

We've left Jamal and Bibi to have some quiet time with their mum and dad. Dave and Menzies and his dad are meeting some of the other refugees, and because Dad's still busy handing out massagers, I'm taking the chance to have a quiet moment myself.

The time is approximately 11.40 am. and I'm proceeding in a westerly direction along the inside of the detention centre fence, gazing out at the stream of cars and buses that are still arriving, and planning a really important letter to Gavin.

*Dear Gavin,*

*Thanks for the encouragement about the job. It went really well and I've learnt a lot.*

*One of the things I've learnt is that sometimes people go to jail just for trying to make things better for the people they love.*

*I know that's what you were doing, Gavin, when you nicked that cuckoo clock. You wanted to show people we were a real criminal family so they wouldn't laugh at Dad behind his back. You didn't realise that Dad is someone who does what he believes is right no matter what other people think. Mum is too.*

*I think you understand that now, Gavin, and I think one day you'll be like that yourself and I'll be very proud of you.*

*I want to be like that too. I've decided to spend my life trying to make things better, even if people laugh at me behind my back and even if I have to go to jail at some point.*

*I've met people who don't ever dream of making things better for other people,*

216

*and I think that really is criminal.*
  *Love,*
  *(Only forty-nine days to go)*
  *Bridget.*